AFTER SHOCK

A Lucy Guardino FBI Thriller

CJ LYONS

AFTER SHOCK

A LUCY GUARDINO FBI THRILLER

CJ LYONS

LEGACY BOOKS

This book is a work of fiction. Any references to historical events, real people, or real locales are used fictitiously. Other names, characters, places, and incidents are the product of the author's imagination, and any resemblance to actual events or locales or persons, living or dead, is entirely coincidental.

Never surrender, never quit the fight.

~Francis Guardino

CHAPTER 1

Now
JANUARY 21, 4:42 P.M.

LUCY GUARDINO HEAVED her body free from the black pit that had been her prison, her bloody handprints a stark contrast to the snow. She rolled over, faceup. The sky was growing dark. Not the complete absence of light that had drowned her when she'd been trapped belowground. Rather, the twilight of a winter's night. A scarlet ribbon of light clung to the hills in the distance, the last remnant of sun that this day would see.

She closed her eyes and rubbed the skin on her neck left raw by the rope. Home. She wanted to go home. To be with Nick and Megan.

How long? How long since her captor had left her? How much time did she have? Snow numbing her body through her wet clothes, her breath coming in shallow gasps, she tried to quiet her thoughts enough to perform the simple calculation.

January. Sun set around five. He'd said his deadline was seven. But how long had it taken her to free herself? How long since he'd left?

How much time did her family have before he killed them?

A bird screeched, shattering the quiet. Lucy opened her eyes. Some kind of owl. Bad omen. Her throat clenched against unbidden laughter, choking it to silence. Even the slight attempt at making a sound burned, her throat scraped raw from almost choking to death down below.

But she hadn't choked to death. Hadn't drowned either. She'd escaped.

Her body shook with cold—all she wore were slacks, a silk blouse, and a thin suit jacket. She was soaked through. But she was alive.

He hadn't intended that. He thought she'd die down in that pit.

Which meant he wasn't infallible. He made mistakes.

The biggest one was threatening her family. Nick. Megan. She had to save them.

Get up! In her mind, her voice was loud, not to be ignored. The barn. She had to make it across the field to the barn. It would be warm there—and she was cold, so very cold. Maybe there'd be a phone. A car. Weapons.

The dog. Panic danced with pain, centered on her left ankle and foot. For a second she couldn't breathe, terror throttling her—as effective as the rope had been earlier. Red spots swirled through her vision and refused to vanish even after she closed her eyes. Oh hell, how could she have forgotten the dog? It would scent her blood, stalk her, finish the job it had begun.

Nick. Megan. Their names were a tonic, easing the turmoil. Thinking of them, she could breathe again. She could put aside the pain—no worse than the pain when she'd had Megan, too late for an epidural. What a blessing that pain had been. So very worth it.

Taking control of her breathing, focusing on nothing except her family, Lucy climbed to her feet. Oh God, it hurts, it hurts so bad. Breathe, she told herself. Just breathe. Nick and Megan are depending on you. You're the only one who can save them.

The pain inched away, waiting for the chance to ambush her again with her next step. She clenched her fists, refusing to lose her momentum. This time she was ready. She took a short hobble-step, balancing on her left toes only long enough to swing her right foot forward.

She staggered across the snow-covered field, leaving a trail of blood behind her. Each step thundered as her left foot touched the ground no matter how briefly. Twice the pain overtook her, forcing her to stop, losing precious time.

Through the haze of misery, she saw Nick's face, the special smile he reserved for their private moments, coaxing her forward. Megan's laugh swirled around her, buoying Lucy up against the tide of pain, and she was able to start moving again.

She breathed through the agony, clinging to thoughts of her family, and the barn—a large metal Quonset-hut structure a hundred yards away—slowly grew closer.

The evening was silent. No distant lights or rumble of cars. Just the whispered sigh of wind through the trees that surrounded the field and the rasp of Lucy's breathing. She wrapped her arms around her chest, trying to generate some heat. Her right hand clasped Megan's bracelet—it had saved her life. She couldn't wait to see Megan, to tell her how her gift had saved them all.

She imagined her daughter's arms—and Nick's as well—hugging her tight, so tight. They'd be all right, she vowed. He wasn't going to harm them. Not tonight. Not ever.

Not while she still drew breath.

She blinked and realized she'd made it. She was at the Quonset-hut barn with its large sliding door, built for farm machinery like combines and tractors. There was a smaller, man-sized door beside the larger one. She reached for the latch but stopped.

Light edged its way around the door. More than light. Sound. The rustle of someone moving around inside.

He was in there. She could end this here and now. Finish it before he ever had a chance to get near her family.

Or should she run? Shape she was in, injured, weak, cold, no weapon—how could she take him on?

She glanced around, hating how much effort it took to force a clear thought through the cold that muddled her mind. The sun was gone, vanished behind the hills to the west, but it wasn't completely dark, thanks to the twilight glow offered by the snow. Across the fields there was nothing except trees.

She had no idea what lay beyond the barn. Perhaps escape. Perhaps her captor's accomplices.

Perhaps the dog.

That made up her mind. She couldn't face that beast again.

Lucy's hand tightened on the latch. He'd made his final mistake, letting her live.

THEN
JANUARY 21, 7:34 A.M.

"Megan! Don't make your dad late." Lucy called up the stairs from the kitchen as she munched on a piece of peanut-butter toast, holding the toast with one hand and unplugging her cell phone from its charger with the other. "Not if you want time to stop by the vet's and see if Zeke's feeling better."

Their orange tabby swirled between her legs, leaving marmalade streaks of hair on Lucy's black slacks as he meowed, pining for his missing canine companion. Lucy would never admit it to anyone, but she missed the exuberant puppy as well.

Zeke, Megan's Australian shepherd, had gotten sick yesterday, with vomiting and diarrhea so bad Lucy and Megan had rushed him to the vet. Poor thing was going through a stage where he ate anything—who knew what he'd chowed down while in the backyard. Seeing Megan so upset, in tears as they'd left Zeke with the veterinarian, was exactly the reason Lucy hadn't wanted any pets in the first place.

It was one of the few times she and Nick had actually fought—and that she'd lost. They'd only been in Pittsburgh a few months, and she was just getting her feet under her in her new job leading the FBI's Sexual Assault Felony Enforcement task force. Nick had his new psychology practice. Megan was juggling school and soccer and making friends. It couldn't have been a worse time to take on the added responsibilities that came with an animal.

So, of course, they'd ended up with two, a dog and a cat, in the space of a week. She still wasn't sure how that'd happened—blamed it on the mild concussion she'd suffered at the time.

Nick bounded through the door to the garage, accompanied by the noise of his Explorer idling. "Megan!" he shouted up the steps.

"I told you I have to cover group tonight, right?" he asked Lucy, stealing a bite from the opposite side of the piece of toast in her mouth while she freed her hands to slip into her suit jacket and smooth stray crumbs from her blouse. She wiped peanut butter from his lip, snagged a quick kiss. Peanut butter and mouthwash, not the best combo.

"Mom's coming to sit, since I have no clue how long this snoozefest in Harrisburg is going to last." Her appointment to the Governor's Task Force on Violent Crime Prevention was meant to be an honor, but so far the monthly meetings had been more about placing blame and whining about budget cuts, and less about taking action. Exactly the kind of meetings she despised.

Megan clomped down the steps, her school bag slung over her shoulder, gym bag with her karate gear in hand. "Why is Grams coming to babysit?" she asked, rushing past Nick and Lucy as if they were the ones dawdling. "You said I could go to the movies with Emma after karate, remember?"

Lucy glanced at Nick, rolling her eyes out of sight of Megan. Ever since she'd turned thirteen Megan seemed to think her parents were addled old folk she could outwit with fast talk and misdirection. Sad thing was, given Lucy and Nick's busy work schedules, Megan's tactics too often worked. "Nice try, but no."

"Mom—"

Nick intervened. "You're not old enough for an R-rated movie."

"But Emma's parents—"

"Aren't the puritanical monsters we are. I know, I know." Lucy ruffled Megan's dark curls, which matched her own, and hugged her daughter, despite Megan's protests. "Besides, it's a school night."

Megan squirmed free. "I don't need a babysitter. I'm thirteen. I should be babysitting other kids."

"We know that. But—" Lucy looked to Nick for help. How to explain that her anxiety had nothing to do with Megan and everything to do with the outside world and the people who inhabited it? Psychopaths like the Zapata drug cartel thugs who'd tried to burn down half of Pittsburgh last month.

"But we would feel better having another adult here with you," Nick said, emphasizing the "another."

Nice touch, Lucy thought. It helped having a clinical psychologist to share the load when negotiating with a teenager.

Although lately it felt like much of Megan's behavior was less about rebellion and more about reestablishing balance to her world. A suspicion confirmed when instead of pulling away from her mother, Megan reached out a hand to stroke the braided black Paracord bracelet she'd given Lucy for Christmas. Megan had made it herself, incorporating a secret touch: the clasp concealed a handcuff key. Something that would have come in handy a few months ago when a serial killer had taken Lucy hostage.

Lucy hated that her daughter thought that way. Hated that she had to. She wore the bracelet every day, not because her duties as supervisory special agent in charge of the FBI's Sexual Assault Felony Enforcement squad put her in danger—99 percent of her time at work was spent behind a desk fighting terminal boredom, not violent felons. She wore it because she wanted Megan to feel secure.

"Besides, your grandmother hasn't seen you in a week. It'll give you two time to catch up."

Since Megan knew exactly how to shamelessly manipulate her maternal grandmother into doing almost anything, she smiled and nodded. "So it'd be okay if Grams took Emma and me to the movie instead of Emma's big sister, right?"

"Wrong," Nick and Lucy chorused.

Megan just grinned. Then her expression turned mournful. "Does Zeke really have to stay another night at the vet's? He's going to be okay, right?"

"Dr. Rouff said he'd be fine," Lucy answered. "She's only keeping him as a precaution."

Really? Nick mouthed. She gave him a small nod as she hugged Megan good-bye, glad that she'd found time to call the vet already this morning. Just like she'd found time to schedule quick trips home during the day yesterday to check on Zeke when he first started acting sluggish and then got sick. Not because she really cared about the rambunctious puppy who was as likely to eat her shoes as his dog food. No, of course not. It was Megan she was worried about.

"You don't fool me, you old softy," Nick whispered as he grabbed Lucy around the waist for another kiss. "You are devoted to that puppy."

Lucy squinched her nose at him. "Hush. You'll blow my image as a kick-ass federal agent. It's the only way I get any respect around here."

Nick chuckled, shaking his head. "Yeah, right."

"Come on, Dad. We're late." Megan waved good-bye and ran out with Nick on her heels.

The door slammed shut behind them. For one rare moment the old Victorian fell silent. Then the heat clicked on, old pipes creaking in protest as steam rattled through them. Lucy glanced around the kitchen with its bright-yellow paint and busy-family-on-the-run Post-it–note decor. She slid her service weapon into the front pocket of her bag for the long drive to Harrisburg, slipped her backup Glock into its ankle holster, grabbed her travel mug of coffee, and headed out the front door.

Lucy always parked her Subaru nose-out in the driveway, since the garage was crammed full of bikes and other junk, leaving only room for one car. Plus she had to leave in the middle of the night more often than Nick—at least she used to. Now that his patient load at the VA's PTSD clinic was climbing, it was a fifty-fifty toss-up who would be called out into the dark hours.

Nick had scraped her Impreza clear of the few inches of overnight snow and started the engine so it would be toasty warm for her. Fifteen years of marriage and he still remembered the little things.

As she walked out to her car, double-checking her bag to make sure she had the files she needed, she reminded herself to try to think of something special to surprise him. Maybe for Valentine's Day she'd kidnap him, take him to a fancy hotel for the night, no phones allowed except to call room service. They could go dancing—Nick loved to dance, and he was good at it. A skill learned growing up in Virginia with its tradition of cotillions, not to mention three sisters to squire to parties.

Smiling at the image of Nick's arms wrapped tight around her, guiding her across a dance floor, she'd reached the hemlocks flanking the driveway when movement came from the shadows.

Lucy spun to face the threat, but she was too late. A man's arm wrapped around her throat.

CHAPTER 2

LUCY EDGED THE barn's door open the slightest crack, straining to see where the man was. Surprise was her only weapon.

The hinges let loose with a creak that split the night. She stepped back, positioning herself behind the door, and held her breath. Maybe he was too far away to hear.

Footfalls sounded. Close, very close. The light inside the barn went out. Lucy braced herself, ready to pounce, knowing she'd only have one chance at this. But there was nowhere to run, nowhere to hide—not moving as slow as she was.

Somewhere inside her a stray spark of warmth gave her strength as she waited in the frigid night air. With it came Nick's voice, chiding her for never being willing to back down from a fight. "You can't always win by outstubborning

19

everyone else," he'd said.

They'd both laughed, knowing perfectly well that that was how Lucy *always* won. She never surrendered, never gave up . . . a trait that had caused more than her fair share of problems both at work and at home.

Nick. She blinked hard, willing him back to the shadows of her mind. Focus, she had to focus. Time this just right.

The door swung open. A man's hand holding a semiautomatic pistol slid into sight. Lucy shoved her entire weight against the door, slamming it shut on his wrist.

The hard edge of the metal door hit him just below the thumb, where it was most vulnerable. He cried out, tried to jerk his arm back inside. Keeping her weight on the door, pinning his hand, she wrenched the weapon from his grasp.

She fumbled the gun between her frozen, numb fingers. Finally got a solid grip on it. Felt so much better having a weapon.

Time to finish this.

Lucy released her weight from the door and threw it open, raising the pistol at the man caught inside the barn. In his effort to pull his hand free, he'd pivoted so that his back was to her, and the darkness almost engulfed him.

"FBI! Hands where I can see them," she commanded. It felt like she was shouting, but her voice barely scratched above a whisper. An aftereffect of almost strangling down in that damn pit. Still loud enough that the man complied— that's what was important.

"On the ground," she ordered, entering the

barn, leaving the door open and keeping her distance so he couldn't rush her. Dim twilight edged through the door, barely enough to make out the strangely shaped shadows of farm machines and the silhouette of the man in front of her.

He stood only six feet away, too close for comfort, but she couldn't risk losing him to the blackness that crowded the rest of the barn. Any farther in and she wouldn't be able to see her own hands holding her weapon, much less her captive.

"I said, get down on the ground," she repeated when he didn't comply. Her voice was swallowed by the darkness, a faint ghost of her usual tone of command.

She reached behind her, fingers brushing the steel wall, searching for the light switch. The barn was warmer than outside, but not by much, making her glad the man still had his back to her and couldn't see the chills shaking her aim.

"You're dead," he said in a snarl that she wasn't sure was a promise or a threat. Didn't matter as long as she was the one with the gun.

She felt a switch and flicked it. The outside light above the door behind her came on. Not much help. Instead of black-on-black darkness, now she could make out grey shadows maybe ten feet inside the door. The farm equipment took on the shape of prehistoric monsters, all claws and straggly arms and squat bodies.

The man made his move, pivoting and lunging at her weapon hand. Lucy rolled with his weight, using her hip to send him up and over, down to the floor. His hand closed over hers, both of them clenching the pistol as he kicked her right foot out from under her and pulled her down on top of him.

Her weight crashed down onto her injured foot. Pain screamed through her. The fight was surreal: arms and legs flailing in shadows, occasionally crossing the sliver of light coming through the door, then vanishing into darkness once again. He grabbed her hair, pounded her face into the cement floor, releasing a gush of blood from her nose. She shot an elbow so hard into his neck that his head whipped back and sent a bunch of hoes and rakes and shovels that had been leaning against the wall clattering to the floor.

Finally, the man caught her from behind in a bear hug, both hands now on top of hers, wrapped around the gun. Her free arm was trapped between his arm and his body as he leaned his weight back, hauling her with him, the pistol rising until she aimed at the ceiling. He braced Lucy's arm against the floor and squirreled his finger around the trigger, pinching her finger as he pulled over and over again.

The sound of gunshots hammered through the space, echoing and reverberating. Hot brass flew from the semiautomatic, pinging against the concrete floor, searing Lucy's hand. One casing tumbled into her jacket, hot against her cold body.

The magazine emptied, and the slide flew back, pinching the man's hand above hers. The pistol was now useless except as a blunt instrument. The man relaxed his grip, and Lucy took advantage, rolling her weight in the opposite direction and twisting, aiming an elbow to his armpit as she scrambled for one of the garden tools.

The air smelled of gunpowder and hay. Lucy's breath came in jagged rasps, each one burning her already raw throat. She shook away any feeling that could distract her, intent on piercing the shadows and delivering the next blow. The man was taller, bigger, stronger, less exhausted—all he had to do was wear her down. Which meant she had to strike, and strike fast.

She grabbed a rake near its working end and aimed it like a claw at his face. The movement broke her free of his stranglehold. She kept rolling onto her feet. Big mistake—she'd forgotten about her left foot. Riding the wave of pain, she planted her foot, braced herself with the rake, and aimed a kick to his solar plexus that had him clutching his gut.

She hopped back, all her weight now on her good leg, groping behind her to lean against the wall and try another kick. Too late, too slow. He was climbing to his feet, half turned away from her, hands lowered as he hauled in a breath.

Lucy took advantage of his pause and swung the rake at his throat, ready to follow up with a jab to his solar plexus. He saw the movement and grabbed the rake from her, sending her flying face-first into the wall, striking a metal circuit breaker box hard enough that the crash rang through the space. Fresh pain brought tears to her eyes as the bones in her nose crunched.

Before she could recover, he grabbed her from behind. She launched her right fist back into his groin, throwing all her weight into it.

"Bitch," he gasped as he released her. She spun around. He was breathing hard, but it was from pain, not exhaustion. She was down to her last reserves of energy.

Lucy had to end this. Now. As he straightened, she pushed off with her good foot, put her head down, and rushed him. She plowed into him, spinning him off balance so that he faced away from her, and shoved him into the side of a large piece of equipment that sat against the opposite wall. Its shadow suggested that it was big and heavy enough to do some damage.

Something at the base of the machine must have caught the man's foot, because he suddenly flipped forward, flying from her grasp. His scream echoed louder than the gunshots. There was a sickening thud of metal meeting flesh, and his scream died.

Lucy couldn't stop her momentum, crashing into him from behind, cringing at the feel of unrelenting metal crunching into the man, her weight pushing his body deeper into the maw of the machinery.

She twisted away, flailing her arms against a darkness so complete she could barely make out the man's silhouette; the machine had swallowed him. Her hand brushed a horizontal metal bar, then hit a sharp curved blade longer than the spread of her fingers.

She hobbled away, panting. The man didn't move, didn't make a noise. The smell of blood and the sour spray of stomach acid filled the air.

She backed against the wall, hitting the edge

of the large sliding door, and finally found the lights. Flicking them on, three bare bulbs hanging from the curved ceiling twenty feet overhead, she was greeted by a macabre melding of man and machine: A huge combine, painted a cheerful spring green. In front of it, several rows of blades, deadly daggers arranged a few inches apart. Impaled on them, one row spiked through his face, a second through his belly, was the man, his blood pooling at his feet.

THEN
10:24 A.M.

Lucy woke, mired in the cotton-packed grogginess of whatever drugs they'd given her. They? He? No, surely there'd been more than one? The void in her memory blindsided her. Terror lanced through her, starting in her gut, then spreading cold throughout her body.

She fought through the haze. Remembered Nick and Megan leaving, walking to her car—then nothing. It took her a minute to connect her senses to her limbs. Weapon— where was her weapon?

Not at her hip. Her feet were bare—socks and boots and backup piece missing.

She pried her eyes open. At least she thought she did. The blackness was so complete that she couldn't tell which way was up. The vertigo triggered a bout of nausea, and she closed her eyes again, focused on her breathing until it passed.

Her hands were bound behind her with zip ties, the plastic cutting into her skin. Tight. Very tight. She grabbed hold of that stray thought racing past, thankful to have one clear thing to concentrate on. Forced her muddied mind to repeat it, seeking truth behind it.

The zip ties were tight. Very tight. Ahh . . . yes. That was actually good—most people didn't realize the tighter they were, the more easily zip ties could be broken when stressed in the right way.

One clear thought led to another as she piecemealed her existence here and now into something she could make sense of. She lay on concrete. Cold. Roughly finished. Basement? Cellar? There was no light, not the faintest crack coming from a window or door. No sounds of the outside world, nor of the inside of a house.

A silence so deep it produced its own echo.

Which meant she was alone. No backup. No one to call for help. No one.

Her body shook with the cold, and she forced herself to return to her inventory. In addition to her weapons, they'd taken her jacket, her belt, her boots and socks, and all her jewelry, including her wedding ring and Megan's bracelet. Left her in her slacks and blouse—thin protection against the cold, but a comfort nonetheless. They needed her alive and unharmed . . . for now.

A quick list of possibilities filled her mind. There was Morgan Ames, the teenage psychopath, daughter of the serial killer Lucy had caught several months ago. But Morgan and Lucy had reached a tentative détente, thanks to Nick. Lucy let Nick counsel Morgan and keep tabs on her while Morgan stayed away from Megan.

So, not Morgan. Her father reaching out from prison? Maybe, but he had enough on his hands with his trial date approaching. The Zapatas, the drug cartel that had attacked Pittsburgh?

Maybe. A definite maybe. Because of Lucy, one of their favorite sons was dead, not to mention a huge distribution pipeline destroyed. Grabbing a federal agent from her own driveway? That had cartel written all over it.

Then why sedate her? Why not just throw her in a car, torture her in some spectacular way destined to go viral on YouTube, and dump her body as a warning?

Not that it might not still come to that . . .The chill of terror returned, her entire body shaking as she fought to push back images of what the Zapatas had done south of the border.

But this felt too . . . civilized? Too meticulous, too elaborate for the Zapatas.

Which brought her back to why? If she understood what they wanted, she could find a way out of this. Who were they? What did they want? Why her?

Without answers, she was helpless.

Before she could roll onto her feet to start exploring her prison and search for escape routes, a man's voice rang out from above.

"The bureau's official policy is no negotiating with terrorists," he said in a calm tone. He wasn't speaking loudly, but the room's strange acoustics made his voice reverberate as if attacking her from all sides. "You need to know two things about me, Special Agent Guardino. First, I'm not a terrorist. And second, this is not a negotiation."

She twisted her body, searching for the source of the voice. Impenetrable blackness greeted her from every direction.

"At seven o'clock—that's in eight hours and thirty-two minutes—your family will either be alive or at least one of them will die cursing your name. Who lives and who dies? That is the last choice you will ever make. Because you will die here today. That I promise."

It was difficult to understand his words, the way his voice echoed and boomed. But as she analyzed the sound, she realized that the space was smaller than she'd thought. And that the voice came from a speaker—there was a faint hum underlying everything he said.

So. He wasn't in here with her. More the pity—a hostage might come in handy when she broke free.

"Who are you?" she shouted, wincing as her own voice bounced back at her. She shuffled her body across the floor, assessing the dimensions of her prison. It only took two moves to find a wall.

"Names are unimportant. What you need to know is that I'm a man of my word and I've done this before. Believe me when I tell you I know the outcome of our little encounter here today. I've already won. There is nothing for me to lose. But there is everything for you to lose. If I need to, I will kill every person you have ever loved. You will listen to their screams, watch them die, and you will be helpless to do anything about it."

Like hell, she thought, bracing herself against the wall. More concrete. Smooth, not cinder block. She pushed herself to a standing position and started to work on the zip ties.

He continued, "It won't come to that. It never does. Your only hope, your family's only hope, is for you to realize I'm telling the truth and give me what I want. You have eight hours and thirty-one minutes left."

There was a faint click, and he was gone. Leaving Lucy in the dark, no idea where she was, no idea who he was, and no idea what the hell he wanted from her.

CHAPTER 3

LUCY SMEARED THE back of her hand against her smashed lip, mixing her own blood with the dead man's.

It was good to finally have light so she could assess her situation. Make sense of it, make a plan. Why did that simple thought seem to take minutes to process?

Cold wind gusting through the barn door left her shivering. It didn't help that she was soaked through and barefoot. Even if she found her boots, she couldn't put them back on, not with one foot swollen and bleeding, bones crunching every time she placed her weight on it. She needed a doctor's attention, probably even a surgeon's, but she couldn't waste time on a

31

distraction like a broken foot; there was too much at stake. Too much she had to take care of before she could take care of herself.

Like saving her family.

She retrieved the rake and gripped its handle, bracing her weight against it, taking the pressure off her foot. Didn't stop the pain. Her body felt like a firing range target after a SWAT team drill: a scattershot of holes and gashes and ragged tears.

Each beat of her heart throbbed through her entire being, pinpointing an assortment of injuries: Knuckles scraped raw. One hand not working quite right. Probably more broken bones. It was hard to breathe with her nose dripping mucus and blood.

Her throat felt swollen to the point that each gasp threatened to strangle her and finish the job the man facedown at her feet had begun. He'd promised that by seven o'clock someone would be dead.

And he'd said he was a man of his word.

What time was it now? Panic surged through her, but she forced herself to take things one step at a time. First, a way to warn her family.

She stared down at the man she'd killed. Grunting with pain, the rake wavering as she balanced it against the concrete floor, she awkwardly searched his pockets with one hand. Contaminating the crime scene. She knew better.

As an FBI supervisory special agent, she'd be called upon to describe and defend each blow of the encounter. It wasn't often an FBI agent was forced to kill a man in close-quarters combat. The brass, the lawyers, the shrinks—they would all be dissecting every second, every decision she made, every step she took today. God, the press—they'd have a field day.

"You sonofabitch," she muttered, long past caring that there was no one alive to hear her. Once again her voice surprised her, emerging as a thin whisper, barely audible even here in the still and quiet barn. It hurt to speak, but no more than any of her other injuries. "Give me something. Car keys, a phone—"

Nothing.

She cursed and straightened, her bad foot throbbing. Red flashes strobed into her vision with each heartbeat. He had to have a phone.

His vehicle. He must have left it in his vehicle.

The cavernous barn was filled with large equipment: the combine, a smaller tractor, various blades and attachments. The door at the opposite end seemed miles away, but she had no choice. There was no phone here inside, nothing to help her reach her family.

As she limped toward the door, shivering at even the thought of returning outside to the cold, anxiety pounded through her, driving her despite the pain. Had he kept his word? Sent his men after Nick? Or had he betrayed her and sent them after Megan? Maybe her mother?

No way of knowing.

She was damned if he had, damned if he hadn't. At least, either way, he was still dead.

She didn't even know his name. A weak

33

rumble of laughter shook her. She clutched the rake tighter, bracing her body with it. Couldn't risk falling. Might never get back up again.

The thought brought more impotent laughter mixed with tears. The sound was sharp, raspy, no louder than a whisper. Yet, despite the pain from her bruised vocal cords, she couldn't stop.

Hysteria. Shock. Not to mention a healthy dose of awe.

Who in their right mind would have predicted that a Pittsburgh soccer mom, an FBI agent with a job meant to keep her chained to a desk, a woman barely five foot five, would have ended her day killing a man with her bare hands?

Sure as hell was the last thing on Lucy's mind when she got up this morning.

THEN
10:52 A.M.

Lucy shivered in the absolute darkness of the prison her kidnapper had left her in. It had been a long time since Lucy had done any tactical training involving close-quarters combat or skills like breaking free from zip ties. Her job as head of the Sexual Assault Felony Enforcement Squad required a different set of talents: managing a multiagency, multidisciplinary task force, investigating cases no one else wanted and playing diplomat to local, state, and fellow federal law enforcement agencies.

Now that 90 percent of the Bureau's resources were dedicated to counterterrorism and financial crimes, the rest of the Pittsburgh field office had dubbed her tiny corner of the building the Island of Misfit Boys. Catching terrorists was so much sexier than chasing pedophiles and serial rapists, but Lucy wouldn't have it any other way. Her people were twice as dedicated and ten times as determined as any other squad in the Bureau. They might not make headlines, but they saved lives.

Despite the long hours at the desk required by her position, Lucy made sure she stayed in shape and kept up with the latest tactics. At least she hoped she had, seeing as her life now depended on it.

Nausea roiled through her gut. Not just her life. Maybe her family's as well.

No. She couldn't think that way. If her kidnapper had Nick or Megan, he would have shown her proof, used it against her. Which meant they were safe. For now. Her only job was to get the hell out of here and keep them that way.

The tight restraints had left her hands numb. Lucy raised them as high as she could and brought her bound wrists down hard against her tailbone. Nothing. This had definitely been easier to do when she was a few years younger.

She shifted position, bracing herself against the wall. The disembodied man—oh, how would she love to disembody him for real—had threatened her family. She allowed her rage, her sense of violation, her fear to flow through her, tightened her muscles and strained her shoulders to raise her arms higher, and brought them down in one quick snapping motion.

The blow rocked through her as the zip ties broke. Free now to explore her prison, she began by walking the perimeter.

The walls and floor were all poured

concrete. The ceiling was high overhead, beyond her reach. From the way sound echoed, she guessed it was concrete as well. She was against a short wall, only about four feet long. If she stood in the center and stretched her arms, she could touch both sides. The corner was a tightly formed ninety degrees, no sign of light or any crack or seam.

She explored the wall with her hands. Above her, as far as she could reach, her fingertips brushed the edge of a pipe. Not metal. PVC. Maybe three or four inches in diameter, judging from the curve. Too small to escape through if she could climb her way up there.

The pipe frightened her more than the darkness. She couldn't hear any sounds coming through it, couldn't see any light edging its way inside.

Was she buried underground? She shook away the panic that came with the thought and kept following her hands as she blindly felt her way along the walls of her prison.

The long wall was only eight feet—nothing on it that she could feel. Another short wall. Another PVC pipe, again above her head, midway along the wall, same as the first.

An almost-forgotten memory sucker-punched her as she imagined how her prison appeared in daylight. Four by eight by at least seven or eight feet high. Poured concrete. Pipes on two sides.

A small cry eluded her control, and she slumped against the final, featureless wall. The echo of her tiny sound of terror pummeled her, and she put her fist into her mouth, biting off any further sounds.

It was her childhood nightmare come to life.

Every neighborhood had its haunted house—the place kids told horror stories about, trying to spook each other with dares to trespass, test their courage. Growing up, Lucy's neighborhood had been no different, only the tragedy that echoed into her and her friends' lives was all too real: a toddler had wandered into a septic tank with an open lid and drowned.

For weeks, Lucy had had night terrors: swimming and smothering in raw sewage like quicksand, pulling her down, down . . .

Panic drove her pulse into a gallop so strong she felt it in her fingertips. Her breathing quickened as well, then she clamped her throat shut, holding it in. Feeling the burn of her lungs fighting for release.

Was that how it would feel? How much air did she have? Even if she found the overhead hatch, could somehow reach it, even if she got the hatch open, would she find anything except a wall of dirt or more concrete trapping her inside?

Surrendering to the need to inhale, she smashed her palm against the nearest wall. A septic tank. Where better to bury someone alive?

Lucy's childhood nightmare. How could he have known?

He didn't, she told herself, pushing away from the walls to explore the floor between them. He couldn't have. A buried septic tank was simply the perfect place to stash someone you don't want anyone to see or hear.

And what better way to dispose of a body?

The man had promised she would die. He just hadn't said how long it would take.

CHAPTER 4

THE BARN STANK of diesel and dried grass. And now death. A simple metal Quonset hut, designed to house tractors and equipment and combine attachments like the one with the wickedly sharp blades. The one with the man's body facedown, impaled against its blades.

Using the rake as a makeshift crutch and bracing herself against the galvanized-steel exterior wall, Lucy hobbled toward the front door. As she made her slow, ungainly progress, she passed the open door she'd entered through, taking one last look outside, across the snow, at the place where she should have died.

The glare of the light above the door made her trail of blood appear black against the white. Empty field—no help there. In fact the only tracks were her bloody footsteps, the man's boot prints, and the tracks of a large dog.

Christ, the dog. Where was the dog?

Terror gripped her, and she stopped, the rake shaking in her hand. She didn't—she couldn't—face the dog. Not again. Her stomach rebelled, and if she'd had anything to vomit, it would have come up. Ignoring the pain, she forced her body to keep moving.

But that didn't stop her from holding her breath, listening hard for the soft thud of the dog's footfalls, the gleeful wheeze of its breathing when it caught sight of its prey, the whoosh of its rush through the air as it prepared to pounce.

She turned her back on the field and the pit beneath it. She needed to get to her family. Now. Before time ran out.

Seven o'clock. He'd said she had until seven. What time was it now?

Her foot brushed against a stray piece of equipment, and she gasped, the pain so swift and overwhelming she almost dropped the rake.

"No time," she muttered, the thought of Nick and Megan a lifeline leading her from the pain. She resumed her circuit of the barn.

Her grip on the rake was weakening, fingers past burning to numb. Only good thing about the cold was that her feet were also numb, as long as she kept weight off her mangled left foot. The threat of the dog was a constant worry, but she'd seen no sign of it while she was dealing with its owner.

Dealing with. She made a choking noise, swallowing blood and finding a loose tooth with the tip of her tongue. Be honest, Lucy. *Killing* its owner.

She'd killed before—been forced to during the Zapata cartel's attack on Pittsburgh last month. But that was at a distance, through the scope of a long gun. Nothing like what she'd done tonight.

The man's final shriek tore through her memory, jarring her. She froze, imagining he wasn't dead, had somehow pushed himself free of the combine blades and now followed her, intent on finishing what he'd started. Killing her. And her family.

If her captor had lied, if he'd been working alone, then she could relax. After all, he was dead, which meant no one left to threaten her loved ones.

If he was working alone. He'd made a big show out of sending texts and talking about others taking orders from him, talked about coordinating everyone to get everything done by seven o'clock, but she'd seen in him an hubris that matched that of the child predators she hunted. Men ensconced in worlds of their own creation, worlds where they held all the power, didn't easily delegate to others. Wouldn't risk losing control over any aspect of their lives.

Her instincts said he was working alone. But

she couldn't risk her family on a gut feeling. She needed to *know* they were safe.

She reached the front wall of the barn, tugged the door open, and was rewarded with the sight of a Jeep Grand Cherokee. She would have shouted for joy if she could've still felt her lips. Victory, though, quickly turned to ash.

The dog, a large rottweiler, trained to kill, was in the Jeep's rear compartment, kenneled inside a crate. It saw her—or smelled her blood, tasted a second chance to finish what its master had started—and began to bark and lunge against the steel walls that trapped it beyond the reach of its prey.

She hated the dog, but she couldn't waste time dealing with it, as long as it was locked up, safely out of her way. She had to overcome a bigger obstacle: the dead man didn't have car keys on him.

She limped to the SUV and opened the door. Climbing inside brought new waves of pain—pulling her weight up onto the seat, twisting to raise her left foot inside, setting it down again as gently as possible. By the time she finished, her jaw was clenched so tight it felt like hot needles driving into her eardrums. Didn't help that the dog, which outweighed Lucy, was throwing its weight back and forth, rocking the Jeep as it howled for release.

The Jeep was an older model. No nav system, no OnStar, no phone. At least not within eyesight.

But—thank you, Lord!—the man had left his

keys dangling from the ignition. Guess he didn't think killing her would take him more than a few minutes. For some reason, the thought made her want to howl in concert with the damn dog.

Her fingers trembling, she turned the key, holding her breath, expecting this to be some kind of trick, a trap.

The dash lit up with bright lights, the radio startling her as it belted Christian death metal, joining with the dog's howls to create a bone-jarring cacophony. But all of her attention was on the dashboard clock.

5:37 it read in blood-red digits.

Lucy added her own whoop of joy to the noise filling the Jeep. Time. She still had time.

If her captor was a man of his word.

She rammed the vehicle into drive, and sped down the dirt lane. Leaving behind the barn and the man she'd killed, she pushed the accelerator, skidding out onto the paved road the farm lane intersected, without even checking for oncoming traffic.

The dog protested from the rear, where its crate shifted and tilted, then thumped back down. She stabbed the radio off, needing all her energy to block out the pain and figure out where the hell she was.

There was no traffic. The road was two lanes, blacktop, twisting and winding with trees on one side and barren fields on the other. No lights, no signs of civilization.

Then she spotted a road sign. Route 51. So close to home. She could have died—body never to be found—and she would have been just a few miles from home. She forced the thought aside. She had to get home, to save Nick and Megan. . .

No. She shook her head, her brain foggy with pain and adrenaline. No. She didn't know for sure where Nick or Megan were, much less who her captor had targeted.

A phone. She needed to reach a phone.

The January night was clear, stars cascading across the sky. They'd bought their Christmas tree from a farm not far from here, she remembered. Nick dunked homemade doughnuts into hot cider at the farmer's stand while she and Megan slurped hot cocoa topped with dabs of marshmallow whip.

She stomped her good foot onto the accelerator, the wind shaking the Jeep. Up ahead a familiar red-and-yellow sign lit up the night, obscuring the stars. Sheetz. A roadside mecca for weary travelers throughout Pennsylvania, promising hot coffee and clean restrooms, but most importantly to Lucy, a phone. She could get help to Nick and Megan.

An eighteen-wheeler coming from the other direction suddenly cut her off, turning left into the Sheetz parking lot ahead of her.

Didn't the idiot driver see her? There was no room to maneuver around the tractor-trailer. She slammed on the brakes, kicking her useless left foot and sending pain howling through her body.

The dog's barking grew frantic, competing with the screech of the tires. The Jeep wobbled and lurched as she yanked the wheel, spotting a narrow opening between the truck's front bumper and the guardrail leading into the convenience store's parking lot. The trucker finally spotted her, hitting his brakes and twisting the wheel until he almost jackknifed.

The Jeep's center of gravity was too high. It finally surrendered, toppling over the guardrail.

Lucy wrenched the wheel. The seat belt and air bags did their job—her body hurled in first one direction, then slapped back against her seat. *No, no, no*, her voice screamed inside her head. This couldn't be happening. She didn't have time . . .

The Jeep skidded to a stop, resting on its passenger side. Lucy hung from the seat belt, her body trying to fall into the other seat against the door that was now the floor of the vehicle.

Other than a slap from the air bag deploying and more muscles wrenched in unnatural directions, Lucy wasn't hurt. She clawed the remnants of the air bag away. The dog whimpered.

She twisted in her seat and tried to push her door open. It didn't move. The sound of the dog's claws skittering against glass echoed through the suddenly quiet vehicle. Had the kennel broken open? She strained to turn to see into the rear.

Was the damn dog clawing its way over the seat even now, ready to finish the job it had started earlier, eager to tear her apart? This time it wouldn't stop at her foot and ankle. It would go for the jugular.

She rammed her weight against the door. Still nothing. Even if she did get it open, it was going to be almost impossible to climb out on her own, not fighting gravity with her smashed-up foot.

She didn't care. She didn't have time for impossible. Not if she was going to save her family.

THEN
11:11 A.M.

She was in a shitload of trouble, Lucy decided, as she paced the interior of her concrete prison. Literally.

She hugged her arms around herself, cursing the fact that she'd dressed in a thin silk blouse for the meeting in Harrisburg rather than her usual layers of fleece. Maybe she'd freeze to death.

Not a bad way to go. She forced the renegade thought aside. No one was dying. Not today. Not with her family in this guy's sights.

Besides, the concrete and dirt she was buried in made for decent insulation. Despite the snow and frigid temperatures outside, she was cold but not freezing.

How much air did she have? She stopped, doing some quick calculations in the impenetrable black . . . No, air wouldn't be a problem, not as long as the outlet pipes were open.

Easy to seal them off, the pessimistic voice continued, cataloguing the number of ways Lucy's kidnapper could kill her. Or hook them up to a vehicle's exhaust pipe, pump carbon monoxide down here. Or fill the place with water—then it'd be a toss-up between drowning and hypothermia.

Or just leave me here to starve.

No, she'd die of thirst first. Didn't matter.

"Not. Going. To. Happen." Lucy's voice ricocheted from wall to wall, surrounding her with the affirmation, driving her doubts away. For now.

He was probably listening. Maybe even watching if he had concealed a thermal-imaging camera in one of the pipes or on the ceiling.

Lucy didn't care. She wasn't playing by his rules. Not with her family's lives at stake.

She continued her exploration of her dungeon. She walked the perimeter again, fingertips touching the outer concrete wall, feet sweeping the ground invisible to her in the dark, searching for anything hidden there. Halfway down the length of the tank, her toe brushed something hard and sharp.

Lucy stopped. She abandoned the anchor of the wall and stooped to feel what her foot had struck. A cinder block. In the center of the floor.

It was just an ordinary cinder block. No hidden compartments with a stash of weapons, a cell phone or radio. Nothing that could help her. It was really too heavy to use as a weapon, but if she had to she would.

She sat on it, face turned up, pondering the blackness above her. There was only one reason why her captor would have left it here.

He'd needed a way to climb out.

Lucy jumped up and balanced on the side of the block. Hard to do in the dark, with nothing to orient her. She wobbled and caught herself with one palm pressed against the wall, the other raised overhead.

Found nothing. Just more empty blackness.

She stepped down, sat on the block again. At five foot five, she should have felt it if the ceiling were seven feet high . . . Yeah, sixty-five inches plus another sixteen or so of arm reach, plus the eight inches of the cinder block . . . She had to do the math twice to be sure, but seven feet was eighty-four inches, and she should have more than cleared that.

Okay, maybe the septic tank was eight feet tall. Made more sense—if her guy was at least six feet tall, he could probably have made it out of a seven foot container without the block. But at eight feet, he'd need a few extra inches, give him leverage to boost the lid open.

When she was a kid, she'd seen two kinds of lids on tanks like these. Big, thick concrete plugs—no way he'd use that, not until he was certain he was finished with her—and slimmer metal or resin hatches that resembled manhole covers. It'd have to be one of those, something he could open from either side.

If he could do it, so could she. Only she'd need more than a few inches to reach it.

She stood the cinder block on its short side, doubling its height. The floor was level enough that it didn't wobble too much. But climbing onto the tiny platform wasn't easy, even with the walls to brace against. She balanced both feet on the eight-inch square and stretched . . .

Twice she ended up falling on her ass, once she caught herself before falling but skinned her shin on the edge of the block, and finally, breathing slow, concentrating on her feet planted just so, raising her hands bit by bit over her head . . . she found the ceiling.

The small victory thrilled through her. She had enough room to plant her palms flat with a bend in her elbow—good, she'd need the extra leverage once she found the hatch.

It couldn't be far. Even if the block had slid to the side after he pushed off it to climb out, the hatch had to be near the center of the tank. Her fingers swept through the darkness. She forced herself to look straight ahead—couldn't see anything above her anyway, and tilting her face up was messing with her precarious balance.

She found two breaks in the flawless concrete: large eyehooks screwed into the concrete about six inches from each other. Stretched her fingers a few inches more and caught the lip of a round structure.

She'd found her escape route.

CHAPTER 5

GRAVITY ALWAYS WINS, Lucy's father had told her when he'd taught her how to ride a bike. He'd said it with a smile as he helped her up off the pavement and back onto her two-wheeler. Dad didn't believe in training wheels, he believed in finding your own way, always getting up no matter how many times you fell.

Never surrender, never quit the fight. Lucy had adopted his motto for her own after he died of lung cancer when she was twelve—fighting until his very last breath.

He hadn't told her gravity was also a bitch—she'd figured that out herself over the years. And right now that bitch stood between Lucy and her family's safety.

She released a scream born of frustration and pain. Or tried to. The only noise she could make with her swollen vocal cords was a muffled whoosh. But the dog's howling from the back of the Jeep more than made up for it.

A man's face appeared at the windshield. Followed quickly by two more men—both teenagers, one wearing a Sheetz uniform. "You okay?"

"Break the glass," she ordered. It emerged as a whisper. She wasn't even sure he'd heard her over the noise of the truck idling a dozen feet away. "Get me out of here."

They turned away, talking among themselves.

One of them, probably the truck driver, older and stouter than the two boys, climbed up to yank on the driver's side door. He got it open, the entire vehicle shaking and shuddering. Cold air rushed inside, chilling parts of Lucy's body that had finally just thawed.

The clock on the dashboard blinked and changed its reading. 6:01. No time to waste.

The dog snarled and growled at the man. His eyes went wide as he looked behind Lucy to the rear compartment. "That dog safe?"

"No. He's not." She felt like snarling herself. It took all her strength to twist her head to look at him, given that she was hanging on her side, only the seat belt digging into her flesh to keep her from falling. "I'm FBI Special Agent Lucy Guardino. I need to use your phone."

Damn, she could barely hear herself. The harder she tried to shout or yell, the more muffled her voice.

"You hurt? Look pretty banged up. What's all that blood on your shirt?"

"Just give me the damn phone!"

"Hold on, the rescue squad's on their way." He vanished from sight.

"I don't need the rescue squad, I need a phone," she cried out in frustration. The last words vanished into the night, inaudible gasps mingled with tears.

At least he left the door open so she could freeze to death. She'd just have to get out of here herself. She grabbed the edge of the doorframe with her good hand and gritted her teeth. This was going to hurt like hell.

She unbuckled her seat belt, letting gravity have its way with her. Bracing her good foot against the center console, she pushed her shoulders and head through the door.

Plan worked too well. She hadn't realized the Jeep wasn't only resting on its passenger side, it also was lying on an incline angled back end down. First rule of close-quarters combat: wherever the head goes, the body follows.

Gravity, the fickle bitch, knew that rule all too well. As soon as Lucy's shoulders cleared the car, she slid headfirst out and over the side, landing in a wave of pain so intense everything went black.

Then
11:43 a.m.

Lucy scrambled back down to the floor of the concrete tank and carefully repositioned the cinder block directly beneath the hatch. She climbed back up, found the septic tank's lid again and explored it with her fingers.

It felt like resin—good, it wouldn't be as heavy as a metal cover. No hinges on this side; it appeared to rely on gravity to keep it in place. Gravity and anything her captor had placed on top of the tank. For all she knew there could be a dozen feet of dirt or several inches of concrete sealing her inside.

No, she thought with determination. He wasn't done with her yet, so he wouldn't have cut off any chance of his reaching her. She hoped.

She pushed against one edge of the cover. Was rewarded as it gave way. A thrill of anticipation fueled her efforts, and she pushed harder. All she needed was to lift the cover above the rim so she could slide it aside.

It can't be this easy. The devil's advocate inside her head sounded a warning. *It must be a trap, some kind of trick.*

Lucy ignored the voice, excited as she tilted the cover up far enough to catch on the top of the tank, releasing a narrow crescent of light into her prison.

She shifted her fingers to the opposite side of the hatch, sliding them into the small gap she'd created, and pushed the cover away from the opening. A few minutes later she was staring into the pale winter sun almost directly overhead. The blue sky surrounding it and cotton-puff clouds floating past were welcome sights.

Okay, now for the fun. Time to see if all those Pilates and core workouts were worth it. She reached through the opening and grabbed onto the rim. It was about two feet wide, plenty of room. Abandoning the security of the cinder block, she swung her legs up to brace against the nearest wall. Then she pulled with her arms as she pushed with her legs, leveraging herself up and out of the black pit.

Sweat covered her, leaving her instantly chilled by the colder temperatures outside. She rolled onto the septic tank's concrete roof and took a moment to blink at the sky, listen to the birds in the distance, and breathe in the crisp, sharp scent of winter.

A shiver rocked her to her feet as she took in her surroundings. She stood in the middle of an empty snow-covered field. Trees surrounded the field on all sides, the closest at least a quarter mile away. The only sign of civilization, other than the septic tank, was a Quonset hut–style barn about a hundred yards away. The barn was large enough to block any view beyond it, but she guessed that out of her sight, on the far side, there would be a road or some kind of drive leading up to it. Which meant civilization.

Her suit jacket lay crumbled at the edge of the packed snow surrounding the buried septic tank. No signs of her parka or bag, but below the jacket she found her socks jumbled up with Megan's Paracord bracelet. She sat, put the jacket on, shoved Megan's bracelet into a pocket, then worked the socks on to her numb feet. Immediately felt better.

She took a step into the snow where the sun glinted off something bright. Her wedding ring, which she slipped on with a kiss to the cold gold—her good-luck ritual—but no signs of her necklace or earrings or boots. No bag, no watch, no phone, no belt, no weapons.

She pictured her takedown—at least how she imagined it had happened. Grab her, inject her with fast-acting sedative, remove any weapons, restrain her, dump her in the trunk of her own car. Less than two minutes' work if you knew what you were doing.

Drive the car to a place where it wouldn't be found, exchange it for another vehicle, drive here.

Yes, there were the tire tracks in the snow leading from the barn to the buried tank. Looked like an SUV or truck. Boot prints and snow packed down—where he must have dumped her while he removed the restraints and did a more thorough search, taking her jewelry, jacket, and socks before replacing the restraints and lowering her into the pit.

Those eyehooks secured to the tank's ceiling—crude pulley system? Maybe it was just one man behind this after all.

She catalogued all the evidence in her mind's eye, but her feet were already protesting the cold, so she sped up to a jog, heading toward the barn. Rolling hills filled the horizon, no signs of a cell tower, no sounds of traffic or civilization. The barn and whatever lay beyond it were her only hope.

A phone. All she needed was a working phone. She had to call Walden, her second-in-command. He'd take it from there. Walden, a wizard of efficiency, would mobilize the local police and get her family into a secure location.

Once they were safe, she could put her energy into finding her captor or captors and figuring out what the hell this was all about. She smiled at the thought, the fresh air and taste of freedom exhilarating. Man of his word, her ass. He dared threaten her family? When she got her hands on him . . .

Her fantasy was interrupted by barking. She spun, trying to place the sound, fantasizing for one brief moment that it was Megan's puppy, Zeke. Then another thought clicked. Zeke wasn't sick; he'd probably been poisoned by her captor. Clearing the way for the attack on her this morning.

The dog barked again. Dogs came with owners, and owners came with cell phones—or vehicles.

Hope fueled her pulse, and she ran faster. She'd escaped her prison, thwarted her captor, would save her family, and then catch the bastard. Be home for dinner early, if she was lucky.

The dog's barking faded into the distance before Lucy could pinpoint its location. It could have belonged to her captor, she knew that, but she was totally exposed and vulnerable here in the field, so she had no choice but to head to the barn.

Besides, if he had a dog keeping guard on her prison, wouldn't he have left it chained near the entrance to the septic tank? Prevent her from escaping in the first place?

Nothing her captor had done made sense. Despite Lucy's joy at escaping, that realization was an itch she couldn't scratch, irritating every nerve ending and leaving the hair at the back of her neck standing upright.

Or maybe that was the cold. Her entire body burned with it, her steps faltering despite her urgency. The barn waited patiently, its galvanized-steel surface a solid, dull presence that promised salvation.

She was only twenty yards from it, close enough to make out its large sliding door and the patches of rust hugging the curve of its roof. The wind was in her face, but she felt, more than heard, a rush coming from behind her.

Just as she turned to look over her shoulder, a large brown dog, mouth bared to reveal all of its teeth, pounced.

CHAPTER 6

LUCY WAS DYING. It was taking much too long, this shredding of body and soul, pain ripping through her from every direction, tearing at her mind, raging through her limbs.

Should never have fought so hard to escape, a contrarian voice echoed through her brain. Drowning or hanging would have been much faster and less painful.

Something tugged at her mauled foot and ankle. Despite the blaze of pain, all she felt was cold.

That's what you get, the voice continued. Just because you can never take the easy way out. Now it's too late. Might as well just give up, let go . . . stop fighting.

Cold, she was so cold. Letting go would be so easy . . .

Never quit the fight. Her father had lived by those words—died by them as well. Lucy remembered how his death had devastated her mother. The void it had left in her life—she'd been Megan's age.

Megan. Her brain stuttered for one infinite moment, putting a face to the name. More than a face, everything. The smell of No More Tears shampoo, the sting of being on the receiving end of a well-rehearsed adolescent eye roll, the pain of every scrape, bruise, illness, vaccine shot . . . everything that was her daughter flooded through Lucy.

With Megan came Nick. God, Nick . . . What had she done? He would approve, she knew, he would forgive her, but how could she have sent that monster after him?

What choice did she have? At least Nick had a fighting chance. More than Lucy's mother or Megan.

She'd killed one man, but who knew how many might still be out there? She had to help her family. Had to reach them. Or at least be at their side to fight. She couldn't abandon them, couldn't give up, had to save them.

Pain like lightning shot through the frozen numbness that gripped her body and mind. Lucy's eyes popped open as she flailed her arms, trying to lunge at an unseen force. Strong hands and stronger bands crisscrossing her chest held her down. Her foot and ankle raged with fire, pain so intense she struggled to hold onto consciousness, her vision blazing black and red and white. The wailing shriek of a wild animal howled in time with the pulses of agony.

"Stop!" she cried out, not knowing who or what she was fighting against. Her voice emerged fainter than a whisper. "How long?"

"Easy now," a man's voice, calm, authoritative, told her. A paramedic. Trying to help. "What's your name?"

"Phone. Get me a phone." Lucy strained to be heard.

"Don't worry, sweetheart. We'll take good care of you. Are you allergic to anything?"

Lucy shook her head, but large foam blocks held it still. The paramedic adjusted a stiff plastic collar around her neck. It held her chin up and rubbed against her already raw jaw. Time, what time was it?

"I need a phone."

He was close enough to hear that. "We'll get you one as soon as we can. Any medical problems?"

"No. Get me a phone."

He turned away, leaving her powerless, strapped to a board. "Splint in place?"

"Good to go."

"On three."

Lucy was jerked off the ground. The medic's face came into sight, then bounced away again. More men, two near her head, one at her feet. She tried to sit up, but the straps circled her chest and belly as well as her arms and legs. Trapped, she was trapped.

"Let me go, I need to go." She wanted to shout, thought she was shouting—how else to get their attention over the roar of pain and the beast howling in harmony? But instead her voice emerged thinner than the night wind. "Let me go."

A bump as they set her down, her foot jostling, releasing another lightning strike. A gasp tore from her.

"We'll get you something for that in just a minute, sweetheart," the man nearest her head assured her. "Just got to get you into the ambulance and call med control."

"Phone," she begged. "There's no time." Her voice barely reached her own ears.

The man gave no sign of hearing her. He was busy looking over his shoulder, talking to someone Lucy couldn't see. It was so hard to think with all this damn noise inside and outside her head. She had to focus. She needed to . . . Someone needed her, she wasn't supposed to be here, she needed to . . .

"Give me a phone!" She mustered every bit of energy. "Now."

They bounced her into the back of an ambulance, one of the men jumping up inside with her, her words swallowed by the noise of the engine and a beeping by her side. One of the doors at her feet slammed shut. The other started to close, then swung open again, another man sticking his head inside.

"That's Lloyd Cramer's Jeep," he said, his

voice loud enough to make Lucy close her eyes in an attempt to lessen the blow. "And one of his damn dogs in the back. Any sign of him?"

"Nope. Just her. No ID. Must be in the Jeep."

Lucy opened her eyes to tell them who she was. Her vision swam, and nausea made her swallow twice before she could find her voice. It still wasn't normal, every word scraped out in a harsh whisper. "I'm Lucy Guardino. FBI. I need a phone."

The door slammed shut before she could finish. The man beside her was leaning over, talking to the driver beyond her vision. If he'd heard her, he gave no sign of it.

Then they were moving, siren wailing, the man busy talking on a radio, reaching across Lucy, adjusting IV tubing running into her arm, inflating the blood-pressure cuff until it felt like a tourniquet, touching her foot and releasing another wave of pain, clamping an oxygen mask over her face, further muffling her attempts to make herself heard.

It was as if he were everywhere at once, the way he used the tight confines of the ambulance, moving with ease like a sailor accustomed to choppy waters. He never stopped, seemed to always have something more to attend to, even once brushing her hair out of her eyes so she could see.

Time, she had no time. How long had she been out? She couldn't move her eyes far enough to see if there was a clock, and the medic moved too fast for her to see his watch. How much time was left before her captor's deadline? Seven o'clock. She had to reach her family before seven.

Lucy fought to speak, to tell him about Nick and Megan and the man out there, hunting for them. She wanted to beg for his help, for a phone, for just one call to send help, but the toll of her injuries and the exhaustion that flowed through her now that adrenaline had evaporated made it impossible for her to form the words coherently in her mind, much less push them past her bruised vocal cords and out her lips.

No words escaped as she fought the pain and lost. Her eyes fluttered shut once more, her only cry for help the release of a single tear.

THEN
11:57 A.M.

The copper taste of terror filled Lucy's mouth as the world around her slowed into a multisensory freeze frame. The air billowed with smoke from the dog's hot breath. This beast was nothing like Megan's playful puppy. This was a killer, its eyes wild and furious.

Snow crunched beneath its paws as it launched itself at her. Lucy's heart raced so fast the beats blurred into a blitz that thrummed through her entire body.

She pivoted to present a smaller target. Powered an elbow into the dog's rib cage. Their momentum threw them to the ground. The dog's teeth snapped in the air beside her ear as she ducked her head down, protecting her neck, relying on primal instincts to keep her alive. Saliva sprayed her as claws dug into her back, ripping through her jacket.

Survival lay in not giving the animal time to clamp its powerful jaws on her. Lucy twisted her body beneath the dog's weight, struggling to protect her head while also aiming blows at the dog's vulnerable spots. It shook off another elbow to its rib cage and snarled as her fingers impacted its eyes. Then she landed a hard knee to its genitals, followed by another kick as she threw the dog off her.

It howled in fury. She scrambled to her feet. Her breath came in gasps. The entire universe had shrunk to a small circle, target-sized: Lucy and the dog. The beast outweighed her, was more powerful. She couldn't win this fight, leaving flight as her only option. No way she could outrun the animal, not for long, but if she could find a weapon, reach the shelter of the barn . . . She'd just planted her right foot when pain tore through her left calf as the dog clamped down with its teeth.

Lucy kicked with all her might. The dog's grip loosened enough for her to slide her calf free, but then it regained a purchase, biting down hard on her foot where it met her ankle. She felt the crunch of bones giving way, the pain so sudden and shocking she fell facedown into the snow.

Lucy cried out in anguish as the animal dragged her closer. She clawed at the ground, found nothing but snow, twisted her body faceup, fighting to sit up and strike at the animal.

The dog held on, not releasing her no matter how she struggled, its baleful gaze fixed upon her, unblinking. Then it tore at her leg with its front claws, her blood billowing into the air, spraying the snow crimson.

Suddenly the blue sky was blotted out by shadow, followed by a man's smiling face.

"Hold," he told the dog. The dog stopped clawing at Lucy but held onto her mangled leg, its jaws a pair of vise-grips. "Good dog." He crouched down beside Lucy.

"Who are you?" Lucy gasped. "What do you want?"

The man was dressed in khakis and a fleece jacket. He had brown hair, brown eyes, nothing to distinguish him at all except his smile. It was a smile in name only: lips curled in the right direction, a few teeth showing, eyes wrinkled in delight. But unlike most smiles, it didn't promise pleasure or happiness. Instead, it was filled with false regret. As if Lucy were a wayward child who'd broken the rules and now faced punishment.

"Who I am is of no consequence." His voice was as devoid of true emotion as his smile. "What I want is for you to understand the futility of your position. I told you there was no way out. I promised you that you would die here. I'm a man of my word. Now do you believe me?"

"Call off your dog."

In answer, the man hit Lucy in the face with a closed fist. The blow was lessened by his position, crouching, balanced on his toes in the snow, but it was still strong enough to send her sprawling to the side, fresh pain exploding in her ankle as her body twisted against the fulcrum of the large dog holding her leg fast in place. She landed facedown, the air knocked out of her, snow filling her nostrils and scratching against her eyes. Before she could move, the man wrenched both her arms behind her and handcuffed her—real handcuffs this time, not plastic zip ties.

The whole thing was a setup, she realized, trying to think clearly through the pain. Designed to do what? Distract her? Demoralize her?

"What do you want?" She hated that the words came out more like a plea than a demand. Sucked in her breath, fought to regain her composure.

"Release," he said. The pressure on her foot vanished—he was talking to the dog, not her.

He hauled her to her feet. She wobbled, unable to place her weight on her left foot as waves of agony swamped her. Nausea overcame her and she fell to the ground, vomiting.

The man stood and watched. The dog sat and watched, panting, its breath billowing in the cold air.

Once Lucy's stomach was empty and the dry heaves had passed, she turned her face, wiped it in the snow, took in a mouthful and spat it out again. The frozen crystals felt good, offering a numb escape from the pain.

A short-lived respite. When he saw she had nothing left to throw up, the man jerked her up once more. Lucy made her body go limp. She wasn't going back down into that black pit, not again. Even with the dog, even with the snow and cold, even with no one to hear her or see her or help, she'd rather die out here in the light than go back to the septic tank.

His answer was to haul her up and shove her forward another step, forcing her weight onto her injured foot. Then he kicked her leg out from under her, toppling her back to the ground. Lightning blazed through her, shattering her thoughts, making it impossible to feel, hear, see anything but pain. The dog sprang forward, excited by the sudden movement. It nosed Lucy's injured foot, its hot saliva mixing with her blood.

"Still some fight left." He pursed his lips and made a disappointed noise. "Okay then. Your choice. I warned you what would happen if you didn't believe me. You just signed a death warrant. Who's going to die, Lucy? Your husband, your daughter, or your mother?"

CHAPTER 7

RIDING FLAT ON her back strapped to a board, unable to even turn her head, was making Lucy carsick. The bright overhead light of the ambulance was impossible to avoid, so she kept her eyes shut, which helped the nausea but made her feel as if she were floating, somewhere outside her body.

"Crank up the heat," the paramedic called to the driver. "She's still hypothermic."

"It's up," the driver yelled back. "Why's she so cold? Wasn't outside that long."

"I don't know. She's soaking wet and has some injuries that don't add up. Like that foot—I never saw a foot and ankle that mangled from getting caught under a brake pedal."

"We're only ten out from the hospital."

They hit a bump, sending a jolt of pain through Lucy's body. It was sharp, yet nowhere near as intense as it had been before. She was so cold. Made it hard to concentrate on anything, including the pain.

She remembered the last time she'd been in an ambulance. Last fall, she'd gotten a few bumps and bruises, and a piece of metal had sliced into her back. Nothing a few stitches hadn't taken care of, yet some people at the office had been upset when she returned to work after leaving the ER. Muttered about her trying to be some kind of superwoman.

Which surprised the hell out of her, since at the time she was searching for a girl kidnapped by a serial killer. If it had been their daughter, wouldn't they have wanted her back on the job?

Funny. Maybe it was because she was a woman. After all, the same people hadn't said anything about Taylor, a junior agent on her squad, coming back to work after breaking his arm that same day. They'd cheered him.

At the time she'd been irritated by any distraction from finding the girl. But later when she had time to think about it and talk it over with Nick, she'd felt sorry for them. People like that, they just kept their heads down, clocked in, clocked out, and went on their dreary way.

Those people—the ones who couldn't understand why she did what she did—they never would have climbed out of that hole in the ground today. Not even once, much less twice.

They didn't realize it had nothing to do with physical strength. It went deeper than that, this need, this hunger, this drive to never give up on anything or anyone—not even herself. Thank God she had it, whatever it was, because without it her family might die.

Her eyes snapped open, squinting against the bright light. What time was it? Nick. Megan. Her mom. She had to warn them.

"Phone," she pleaded once again. But her voice was even softer than before. Her mouth was parched by the oxygen blowing in—it tasted sweet, like when she'd blown up a bunch of balloons for Megan's birthday party. She licked her lips and tried again. "Phone. I need a phone."

The paramedic leaned over her, shielding her from the light. "I know you're cold," he said, misunderstanding her muffled whisper. He tucked a foil blanket closer around her body. "Hang on, we're almost there."

She tried to shake her head no, but he'd already turned away and the cervical collar and restraints holding her in place on the backboard prevented her from even that small movement.

Inside her head she screamed in frustration, but the only noise she could actually make escaped as a defeated whimper.

THEN
12:19 P.M.

Lucy stopped struggling and lay back in the snow. She stared at the man, focusing all her energy on him. What did he want? The thought reverberated through her. He'd threatened her family again. This time he sounded serious— too damn serious.

"I'll do whatever you want." She forced her voice to stay level and calm, a promise, not a plea. "Just tell me what you want."

It took a moment, but finally he nodded. "Fine. Let's start by getting you back inside your lovely accommodations."

The pit. Her prison. No. She remembered his earlier promise. Her coffin.

With her leg out of commission, the dog waiting to pounce, and the man with unknown weapons or accomplices to back up his threats, what choice did she have? Besides, she'd escaped once; she could do it again.

She hoped.

This time he helped her to her feet and let her lean on him to protect her injured foot. They performed a bizarre three-legged walk back to the opening of the septic tank. The dog followed alongside, occasionally turning its head to fix Lucy with a menacing glare, but otherwise keeping its distance.

The man sat Lucy down near the opening to the pit and rummaged through a backpack. She fantasized about pushing him down into the tank, making another run for it, but he was never close enough. And of course there was the damn dog.

The man glanced over his shoulder at her, a twisted smile on his face, and Lucy knew he'd put his back to her to see if she'd succumb to temptation and try something. More mind games. She was sick of them.

"Remember that DC journalist who vanished a few years ago? The one investigating the senator?" he asked with a grin. Just two folks, making casual conversation, his posture said. "All they found was his Mini Cooper parked by a lake. Three years and no trace."

He held a climbing rope loosely in his hands, turned to face her. "That was me. It's what I do. Make people vanish. Forever."

She tried to tune him out and use her precious time above ground to analyze her surroundings. The man and dog had come from the opposite direction—their path cut across the far edge of the field from a thick stand of pines and hemlocks.

Strange place to park a vehicle—the trees

stretched as far as she could see. Maybe a logging road? Then she spotted the binoculars inside the man's pack. Bastard. He'd watched her escape—probably via a camera concealed inside one of the pipes. Waited for her. Just to set the dog loose and bring her down.

Games. That's what this man lived for. No matter what he told her, she needed to remember that this was all just a game to him. Stimulation, adrenaline, a sense of power, control . . . that's what fed him. He enjoyed competition—as long as he won.

She hid her smile. She might not know what the man wanted, but she knew what he needed: victory. To be the victor. She would use that.

"You have a decision to make, Lucy," he said. "Think of all the questions your disappearance will leave. No closure, not for your family. How many hours, how many years will they spend searching, wondering? Maybe I could drop a few hints—a secret bank account, evidence of an affair—"

Lucy jerked at that, unable to stop the movement. No way would Nick ever believe she'd been unfaithful. Never. But just raising the question, how painful—and he'd never have an answer. And Megan. What would happen to Megan?

Nick would do a great job raising her alone—he had more maternal instincts than Lucy. Something she always felt guilty about. And they'd have each other.

She blinked, stared into the sun. No. She couldn't give up, couldn't think like that. She was going to get out of this. She wasn't going to let this anonymous SOB take her family from her. No way in hell.

The man uncoiled the length of climbing rope and wrapped it around her chest and beneath her arms. She heard the click of a carabiner, then he leaned into the opening to the pit and worked the rope through the hooks in the ceiling.

It took him awhile to lower her into the tank, but he didn't seem to mind. She thought of the time and effort he was taking. Protecting her leg—the leg that he'd caused to be injured in the first place. Trying to buy her trust? Keeping her emotionally off balance, more likely.

She sat in the shadows on the concrete floor, unable to see him even when she craned her neck far enough back to view the opening. He hadn't sealed her in again, but he hadn't joined her either. Was he sending the dog down, locking that beast in with her?

The thought brought more fear than she

wanted to acknowledge. Not just fear of the animal, fear of her absolute lack of control. Feeling powerless was a mere eyelash away from feeling hopeless, and she couldn't afford to go there. She needed to keep hold of hope, no matter how desperate. Without it, she was doomed—and he was still a threat to her family.

The fact that he hadn't replaced the lid, the sunlight that shone down through the narrow opening, the sound of the birds in the distance—these all kept her hope alive.

Then a shadow blocked the light. He lowered himself into the pit, thudding to a landing behind her. His hands came down on her shoulders. "Shall we get started?"

No, she wanted to scream. But she kept silent and still. Waiting. It was his game, his move.

"Do you have any idea how special you are?" he asked. "You see," he said as if she'd answered him, "I have a friend who discovered a vulnerability in the Department of Justice's security software. Actually, there are quite a number of vulnerabilities, which is why the FBI built an entire center in West Virginia devoted to creating a new and improved system, complete with Nextgen biometric security."

She wished she could see him. Faces told

so much more of the story than a voice in the dark.

"So here I am with a back door into the old DOJ network, and there you guys are, ready to move everything into the cyber equivalent of Fort Knox. Which means I need to move fast. Find someone with high enough clearance to access the mainframe so my friend can perform his magic.

"We started with hundreds of potential candidates. Winnowed them out. They had to be from a field office in a city large enough that if they went missing for a few hours no one would notice, yet small enough that we'd be able to breach their security. Had to have administrative privileges on the computer system. They had to be vulnerable. Married. Preferably a woman. With a husband, child, mother to protect. Young enough that they'd be eager to live, experienced enough that they'd know when to cut their losses."

His voice dropped with an edge of excitement, almost sexual. "And then we found you, Lucy. What a treasure trove you turned out to be. All those news stories on you, including photos of your husband and a glimpse of your daughter. Your dear mother living close-by, all alone in the house you grew up in. Not to mention how lucrative the job became once I dangled your name in the right circles.

"Let's see." His voice upticked, and she knew he was counting on his fingers. "My original clients are paying five million to have a back door into the new database. A few mob guys ponied up another two million to gain access to the confidential informant list as well as the undercover database.

"Then came the Zapatas. Do you have any idea how much those people hate you for what you did, destroying their North American operations last month? Not to mention killing their favorite son. Ten million if you die quickly, twenty if I take my time."

He paused, let that sink in. Lucy honed in on his voice, searching for any change in his breathing or pitch that would indicate he was bluffing. She didn't hear any. He was telling the truth.

"Hope you don't think me greedy." He ruffled her hair with his fingers, knelt behind her, and placed his mouth right next to her ear. "But I'm planning to take my time."

CHAPTER 8

"FORTY-YEAR-OLD FEMALE, restrained driver, rollover MVA," the medic called out as they wheeled Lucy into the ER's trauma room. He'd added two years to her age, but that didn't even bother her. All she wanted was for everyone to stop talking long enough to hear her and get her a goddamned phone.

Her fear had been replaced by frustration, which had morphed into fury. Bad enough to be hauled from one place to another like a loaf of bread, but to be tied down and ignored?

Another lift and bump as the medic finished his report and they moved her onto the hospital's stretcher. Men and women appeared and disappeared in her vision as they cut off her clothing, replaced the medics' monitor leads, adjusted her oxygen mask, checked her vitals, started another IV and drew blood, listened to her heart and lungs, ran cold jelly and an ultrasound over her belly, took X-rays of her neck and chest and foot, all the while poking and prodding every inch of her body.

There had to be a clock in the room, but she couldn't see it from her position, restrained to the backboard. What time was it?

The doctors and nurses talked above her and around her, their words sounding like some kind of strange foreign tongue as they circled her captive body like sharks in a feeding frenzy. She thought she had a chance to make herself heard when one of them bent to shine a light in her eyes, but then his partner called to him from the foot of the bed and he was gone.

"Hey, did you see this?" one of the doctors said, his voice tight with excitement. He stood at her foot, and she braced herself against the pain that his touch was about to bring. "Open metatarsal fractures, ankle and calf basically shredded. Thought this was an MVA?"

"There are ligature marks on her wrists and neck," a woman's voice said from beyond Lucy's vision.

"Let's call Three Rivers about that foot—it's going to take a vascular repair. We might have to LifeFlight her over there," an older man said as he examined Lucy's foot, releasing a fresh wave of anguish. The machine monitoring her heart rate sang out in a staccato beat. "No. Wait. Are those tooth marks?"

As they talked *about* her instead of *to* her, Lucy was busy working one hand free of the Velcro restraints. The nurses had replaced her clothing with a hospital gown and had her warming under heat lamps. As she thawed, she felt more of the aches and pains that barraged her body, but her focus also returned.

Once her hand was free, she watched for the next person to come close. It was a woman in scrubs. As she reached to adjust Lucy's IV, Lucy snaked her fingers around the woman's wrist and squeezed hard.

"Give me a phone," she said, the words scraping raw against her vocal cords.

The woman patted her arm as if Lucy were a child. But she did lean forward to listen. "What happened to you, honey? It's okay. You're safe here."

Before Lucy could answer, the two men abandoned their examination of her foot and approached the head of the bed from the opposite side.

"C-spine clear?" a man asked someone across the room.

"Looks good."

The sound of Velcro ripping filled Lucy's ears as the cervical collar and restraints were removed from her head. The man pushed his fingers against her neck bones. "Anything hurt?"

"No," Lucy said, trying to crane her head free so she could read the clock she'd glimpsed on the wall beyond him. What time was it?

He frowned, but the nurse repeated for her. "She says no."

He released his grip on her head, and finally she could turn far enough to see the clock. 6:47. Still time, but not much. She needed to contact Walden, get him to send local police to protect her family. Now.

Both men leaned forward, hovering just above Lucy's face. One of them removed the damn oxygen mask. "Okay then, what happened?"

Finally, someone to listen to her. Lucy mustered every ounce of command presence and forced it all into her shredded voice. "I'm an FBI agent. Get me a phone. Time's running out."

The nurse's eyes went wide. She jerked back, and Lucy thought maybe she was reaching for a phone, but the older man said, "First, I need to know if a dog is responsible for your ankle and foot injuries."

Lucy nodded. "Forget the dog. Lives are at stake. I need to warn them."

"How long ago did the dog attack you?"

Who the hell cared? She needed to get help to Nick and Megan, warn the FBI about the attack on their computers. "People will die if you don't get me a phone. Now."

Her voice was fading, but something in her face must have convinced the nurse, who said, "Let me grab my cell for you."

"How long?" the man repeated.

Lucy shrugged, regretted the movement. Did they have any idea how painful lying on a slab of wood felt after being banged up? "Don't know."

She'd escaped the septic tank the first time a few hours after the man had taken her, but she'd been knocked out part of that time . . . The sun had been almost directly overhead—she remembered that—before the dog . . . She flinched at the memory of the pain. "Around noon. I think."

She pivoted away from the doctors, ignoring the pain that lanced through her leg with the movement. Glanced at the clock. 6:49.

"Get me the phone. Or call the FBI office. Please, you don't understand—time is running out." Her voice faded before she could finish.

Didn't matter, the doctors had turned their backs to her, eyeing the X-rays once again. "Damn. That's way too long. Open fracture, contaminated, dog bite . . ."

The younger man moved back down to her foot, pressed one finger against it for a long moment, then released it. "Delayed cap refill, circulation's compromised. She'll probably lose it."

"Still, we should let the surgeons decide," the older man said.

"I'll give them a call, see if they want to transfer her to Three Rivers." Three Rivers Medical Center was one of Pittsburgh's major trauma centers. Sounded like this small community hospital wasn't equipped to deal with her injuries—least of her worries.

The second hand on the clock wouldn't stop its relentless movement. 6:50.

"Forget the foot," Lucy tried to shout. She pulled herself up to a sitting position and immediately wished she hadn't. Her vision blurred with a wave of dizziness, but she had their attention again. Where the hell was the woman who'd promised the phone? "I need the FBI. Now."

Before the men could answer, the woman returned—along with a sheriff's deputy. Relief surged through Lucy. She just needed to hold on for another minute or two, long enough to get word out to her team. They'd take care of Nick and her family.

She turned to the deputy. His expression was dour. No surprise. Locals didn't like messing with anything federal—and she knew right now she didn't look like any FBI agent they'd seen before. Didn't matter. As long as he listened and called Walden. Walden would take it from there.

"This the woman who crashed Lloyd Cramer's Jeep?" he asked.

"She says she's an FBI agent," the nurse said.

"You see any ID?" Before anyone could answer, he handcuffed Lucy's wrist to the bed rail.

Lucy jerked against the restraints in surprise. "Take these off."

"Whoever she is, I'm not taking any chances," the deputy said. "And there won't be any phone calls until we get to the bottom of this."

"Bottom of what?" the younger doctor asked.

"Bottom of whoever killed Lloyd. I just

found his body back at his barn. Someone skewered his face on a combine blade."

THEN
2:31 P.M.

The man was silent, giving Lucy plenty of time to think. He wanted her to imagine all the myriad ways he could torture her before killing her, taking his time, keeping her alive until she begged for release.

Hell with that.

She wasn't playing by his rules. Or his timeline. She knew how this would end.

She also knew how to save her family.

Who cared about the database of pedophiles and predators? She'd caught them before, she'd catch them again—or someone would.

She gave him the damn password.

Behind her, he stirred in surprise. She almost smiled. "What was that?"

She repeated the string of numbers and letters. They were easy to remember: the date and abbreviation of the city where Megan had been conceived. Something no one except her would know—and maybe Nick, but he was awful with dates. "It's the passcode."

His breath echoed through the dark chamber. Then silence.

Suddenly he was right behind her, his arms snaking through hers to pull her body upright, pressed against his. Her left foot hit the floor with the unexpected movement. She gasped in pain.

But not much fear. Now that he had what he wanted, he'd kill her. But her family would live. There was nothing for him to gain by hurting them—a sociopath like him, it was all about getting what he wanted. And she'd given it to him.

Time to die.

She waited, limp in his arms, balancing her weight on her good foot. Knife to the throat? Gunshot to the head? No, he was greedy, he'd take it slow. Didn't really matter. He might have gotten what he wanted, but so had she. He thought she'd given up, that he'd won. Wrong. She'd won: her family was safe.

He slid one hand free, palm beneath her left breast, against her heart. Nothing sexual about his touch, more clinical. His arms were well muscled, not straining as he supported her weight. His breath came in slow, hot waves, brushing the top of her head as he effortlessly held her in place.

Then he dropped her. Pain screamed through her foot. She choked back her shriek, but couldn't stop the whimper that emerged.

"You disappoint me, Lucy." His voice was smooth, a stiletto that cut through her calm. "Don't waste my time. We only have until seven."

He'd mentioned that deadline earlier. What happened at seven?

"I gave you what you wanted," she protested.

"I told you what would happen if you disappointed me. I told you I'm a man of my word." He sounded betrayed.

She struggled to get beyond the pain reverberating through her body. Shifted her weight away from her injured foot. Then froze as he leveraged his booted foot against her bloody one. He didn't press down. Just held it there, a silent threat.

"Do you think I'm stupid?" he demanded. "I study my subjects, know everything about them. I know the wrong passcode will lock the system down, send a security alert. And I know you, Lucy. The way you saved all those children from the hospital bombing. How you never give up on a victim, even tracking that serial killer years after everyone thought he was dead."

He let up on her foot. She leaned away, bracing herself, knowing he was toying with her.

"You're smarter than any serial killer," she said, trying an appeal to his vanity. "I knew better than to resist. The password is the correct one. I would never try to trick you, not with my family's lives at stake."

He crouched behind her, his arms stroking her shoulders and arms, tracing the lines of her body in the darkness. She shivered, straining to anticipate his next tactic. How could she convince him that he had won?

"No," he finally said, his hand caressing her injured foot. His touch was gentle, barely brushing the torn skin and mangled bones beneath it. Still more than enough to send a shock wave of pain through her body. "You would never give up this easily."

He stood once more, stepping back, abandoning her on the floor. A bright light seared through the darkness—his phone a few feet in front of her. A slide show of images played across it. Her mother. Nick. Megan.

"No," she gasped. "I gave you what you wanted. Please, no."

"I told you what would happen if you disappointed me, Lucy." His tone was fatherly, chiding a wayward child. "I'm a man of my word."

The images rotated like a roulette wheel.

"Your choice, Lucy. Which one will die?"

CHAPTER 9

Now
6:56 P.M.

"I'LL NEED ALL her possessions and clothes bagged for evidence," the deputy told the ER staff. Lucy rattled the handcuffs to get his attention.

"FBI," she mouthed, cursing her stolen voice. But there was still hope. If she could get him to call the FBI, they'd verify who she was—it would take longer than calling Walden directly, but she'd have to risk it. What choice did she have?

"I'll call them and get the detectives down here to do an interview," he told her. His expression was strained: a simple MVA turned into a homicide investigation was less than routine for a weeknight's patrol. It was clear he was trying to do everything by the book, but Lucy needed him to throw the book out.

She rattled the cuffs again. The deputy bent close. "The man?" she whispered. "Cramer?"

"If you are who you say you are, then you know I can't question you until you've been read your rights and the doctors clear you. And if you aren't, well, we'll just wait for the detectives. Nothing's getting thrown out on a technicality, not on my watch."

Lucy shook her head, frustrated that he didn't understand. She took a breath, trying to bolster her voice. Decided to go ahead and play the role of the victim, hoping he'd respond better than he had to her earlier demands. "He threatened my family. Please. Check them."

The more she tried to talk, the more it felt like she was being choked all over again.

He gave her one of those single-jerk-of-the-chin cop nods that could mean yes or could mean no, turned to speak into his radio, then left to join the doctors just outside the open door to the room, beyond her hearing.

She lay back on the stretcher and closed her eyes, blocking out the light blaring down into her face, distancing herself from the pain.

She glanced at the clock. Panic ripped through her, twisting her gut.

7:00. Time was up.

If she was wrong and the man who'd kidnapped her hadn't been working alone, then his partners could be anywhere. He'd left her to die in the pit hours ago. Plenty of time for his accomplices to find her family and infiltrate the FBI's computer system with her passcode.

Nick could already be dead. Her stomach clenched, and for a moment she couldn't breathe. Fear had a stranglehold on her chest. Her heart thudded so hard and fast it set off the alarm on the monitor behind her.

"Are you okay?" a nurse asked.

Lucy opened her eyes and nodded. The nurse didn't see the lie; she was busy checking her vitals on the monitor.

How long since the man had left her to die in the tank? No, that wasn't the right question. The right question was: where had he gone first?

If what he'd told her was the truth, then he'd need a computer that was part of a law enforcement network, tied to the National Crime Information Center and with admin privileges. It didn't have to be an FBI or DOJ computer, but it needed to be more than a mobile data terminal like what the deputy had in his vehicle. No way would the man be able to physically breach the FBI's field office in Pittsburgh. But a computer at a police station would work.

Her gaze centered on the deputy. He still hovered near the door, frowning, one hand on his weapon, as he talked to her doctors. Why hadn't he already called the FBI? Why hadn't he asked more questions? Miranda be damned. She was a federal agent, a man was dead, you'd think he'd want to know something here and now rather than waiting for a detective.

Maybe he was working with her captor. Or

101

maybe her captor was law enforcement. He'd said he had a schedule to meet. Seven o'clock. Maybe it was a work schedule, starting a shift that would give him access to the computer and, through it, the DOJ database?

Or maybe the deputy was just an unimaginative cop, content to do his business without getting involved in federal messes best left to the brass and detectives. Her mind whirled with suspicions and second guesses.

It didn't matter. She needed a phone—one call to Walden, to make sure her family was safe, and she could relax, let the doctors do their work, and let the rest sort itself out.

She glanced at the nurse. She'd been sympathetic, she'd come so close to giving Lucy a phone. A phone that Lucy saw was still in the pocket of the nurse's lab coat. She just needed to get her alone for a minute.

Lucy tapped on the bed rail with the handcuff and nodded to the nurse when she turned around. "Need to pee," she whispered.

"They're talking to the surgeons at Three Rivers about LifeFlighting you there—it's the best hope for your leg. The deputy is trying to figure out what to do with you if they do. Either way, you need surgery. They'll put a catheter in there."

Lucy shook her head. "Can't hold it."

The nurse nodded, patted her shoulder, and went to join the men. One of the doctors left, and the other shrugged at the nurse before following him from the room. Lucy hoped that shrug didn't mean they wanted the nurse to put the catheter in here, or worse, a bedpan—her best bet was if the nurse took her to use a restroom.

The nurse kept talking to the deputy, giving Lucy time to sit back up and assess her situation. Naked except for a hospital gown, her left foot swathed in bandages and an ACE wrap holding a splint in place, another splint on her left hand . . . not much in the way of assets. She didn't even have Megan's bracelet any longer—it, along with everything else she'd worn, was now in brown paper bags in the hands of the deputy.

She glanced at her left hand. Her wedding ring was gone—she vaguely recalled the younger doctor cutting it off during the frenzy of her arrival. Because of the way her hand and fingers had swollen. Boxer's fracture, he'd said.

Her lucky charm. She couldn't stop staring at her naked ring finger, barely visible beyond the edge of the splint. For some reason losing her ring made her even more fearful that something terrible had happened to Nick. Magical thinking, he often chided her—usually with a laugh that his uber-rational wife could be so superstitious.

Superstition or not, the panic was real enough. She needed to get out of here. Now.

The nurse left and returned a minute later with a wheelchair.

"It's not like she's going anywhere. Not with that foot," she said to the deputy as she transferred the bag of IV fluids to a pole attached to the back of the wheelchair. Lucy couldn't help but think that pole would make a good weapon. "And the bathroom is right there." She nodded to a door on the opposite side of the room.

The deputy went to check it out himself, ensuring there were no weapons and no means for Lucy to escape. At least that's what she'd be looking for if she were in his shoes.

"Okay, okay," he told the nurse. "By the time you're back, hopefully the supervisor will be here. I have a call in to the FBI about her. They're going to call back." The deputy sounded irritated that Lucy was still his burden to bear, but at least he had contacted the Bureau—or claimed he had. He unlocked Lucy's handcuffs and returned them to his duty belt.

"My family?" she asked.

"The person I spoke with at the FBI said once they verified your identity, they'd send someone out."

Lucy shook her head. That would take too long. Why couldn't he understand that they were out of time? "Call Don Burroughs. Detective, Major Crimes, Pittsburgh Police. Ask him to send someone. Now."

That earned her another scowl, but it seemed like he was thawing, actually beginning to believe. "You better not be yanking my chain, lady—"

"I'm not."

"All right." He turned to the nurse. "I'll be right outside." Glared at Lucy. "Making *another* call."

The nurse lowered the bed rail and helped Lucy swing her legs over the side. Her left foot felt like a deadweight, tugging at her body as if trying to escape.

"You okay?" the nurse asked. Lucy nodded, and the nurse guided her into a standing position, braced against the bed, her injured foot off the floor. Then the nurse added a second hospital gown, draping it from back to front, returning to Lucy a small amount of dignity, before sliding the wheelchair into place behind her.

Lucy slumped into the chair and let the nurse lift her leg onto the padded footrest. The exertion had left her drenched with sweat and feeling flushed. Hard to believe that a short while ago she'd been freezing.

The nurse pushed her into the small restroom. Before she could help Lucy up onto the toilet, Lucy made a grab for the nurse's phone.

She snagged it from the nurse's pocket, but her movement was clumsy, lacking the finesse she needed to hide it. The nurse whirled. "What do you think you're doing?"

THEN
3:12 P.M.

He stopped the slide show on Megan's image. Lucy sat up straight, gaze lasered in on her daughter's photo. She was not going to let this man hurt her family. Not an option.

She was going to kill him. Lucy had no idea how, but the thought brought with it a certainty that dulled all pain.

He sensed her shift in mood. His foot stomped down on hers. Her shriek echoed through the space for what felt like hours. By the time the sounds died, she was facedown on the floor, barely able to breathe, the cold concrete freezing her tears.

"I gave you what you wanted," she pled. "Do whatever you want with me, leave my family alone." Her words emerged in a fever-rush of anguish and fear.

Then she saw. Instead of focusing on the big picture of how to save her family, she needed to answer the smaller question: what did he want, right here, right now?

He wanted the pain to distract her. No. More than that, he wanted it to break her. Wanted her to surrender to it. To him.

He wanted to emerge from here the victor.

As much as she wanted the pain to stop, she

realized she could use it.

"Please," she begged, no longer fighting the tears. She watched his face in the dim light, trying to read his expression. His eyes widened slightly, just for a moment, and his lips curled in a genuine smile. Finally, a glimpse of the true monster—he enjoyed her pain, but even more, he relished her loss of control.

Now she knew what the beast fed on. Just had to figure out how to keep him happy long enough for her to kill him.

He crouched down beside her again. "Megan's the easy choice," he said in a conversational tone. He softly stroked her hair away from her eyes. "After all, Nick can always have more kids. Let's see . . . she's in English now. That gives my guys time to grab her when classes change in nine minutes."

"No." Lucy had to fight to keep the anger from her voice, to reveal only her pain. "Please. No."

Her entire body shook—cold and pain and adrenaline taking their toll. She lay on her back in the growing shadows that filled the pit, the cerulean sky dancing at the edge of her vision. Freedom. She couldn't let it distract her, had to think only of keeping this madman happy.

"You're right. Best to save Megan for last. Besides, she's easy to get to. Any time." He pursed his lips as if concentrating, consulted his phone once more. "Let's see. Your mom's at a planning committee for the church bazaar. And then she'll be meeting her gentleman friend, Charlie, for an early-bird dinner and bowling. Did she tell you, she bowled a one-eighty last week?"

Lucy let the shakes devour her body, released herself to her tears. Snot poured from her nose, and she turned her face into her shoulder to wipe it clean. Closed her eyes for an instant, hiding her triumph.

Bastard wasn't all-seeing, all-powerful. He didn't know her mom had canceled her plans with Charlie to babysit Megan tonight. Her mom wouldn't be anywhere near her own home this afternoon; she'd be coming into the city to Lucy's house. Could she take the chance, send him to Mom's house?

No. Too risky—he obviously had someone following her. They'd know when she left for Lucy's place.

"Not your mom?" His tone was a strange mix of surprise and pleasure. "I'd actually thought you would have chosen her. She's old, already had her chance at a family, happiness. So it's Nick? Really?"

Nick. Yes. He was at the VA today instead of his private office. He'd be surrounded all day, and into the night since he had group. Protected by his patients, soldiers—young, fit, ready for action.

"Lucy? I need to know. Who do you want me to kill? Is it Nick? Megan? Or your mom?" The man sounded impatient, as if Lucy had been dawdling for no good reason.

Lucy rolled her face back up to the thin slice of sky, keeping her expression blank. Stray tears coated her eyelashes, coloring the world with rainbows as she blinked. Her face was numb, her body numb, and she used that to her advantage.

He leaned forward, his face blocking the sky, creating her world. Master of the universe.

For now. Bastard.

She buried her fury beneath the numbness. "Please. I gave you what you wanted. That's the real code. I promise." She was sobbing again, tears warming her frozen skin. "It's the day Megan was conceived. How could I make that up?" Again, the glint of satisfaction in his eyes. Good.

His gaze searched hers. Then he abruptly stood, towering over her. "Answer me, Lucy." He planted his booted foot over her injured one and shifted his weight down.

The blissful numbness vanished in a tsunami of pain, swamping all conscious thought. Lucy couldn't restrain her scream. It echoed through the small space, escaped into the empty sky so far overhead, then disappeared.

"Who's it going to be, Lucy? Who's going to die?"

He applied more pressure to her ankle. Lucy's body jackknifed upright, her shoulders straining against the handcuffs as another shriek escaped. He removed his boot. Her pants leg was shredded, the black fabric looking like soot caught in a mass of blood and mangled tissue. Nothing remained of her sock, and she swore she saw the glint of bone in the ugly gaping wound that extended from her shin down to her foot.

All this filled her vision in the time it took for her scream to consume all the breath in her body. She fell back, gasping.

He raised his boot high, ready to stomp down with all his weight.

"No!" she cried. "Nick! Take Nick."

CHAPTER 10

LUCY CLOSED HER fist around the phone, but the nurse easily wrested it away. "Please. I need to talk to the FBI."

The nurse looked at her skeptically. "Deputy Renfew said he'd already called."

"And is waiting to hear back from the duty agent. My family is in danger. They may not have time."

The nurse squinted at Lucy, then the door, and finally nodded. "But I'll dial, and we keep it on speaker."

Lucy gave her Walden's direct number. When he answered, the nurse took over. "This is Mary Townsend, a nurse in the ER at Riverside Community Hospital. To whom am I speaking?"

"FBI Special Agent Isaac Walden. What do you need?"

Never had Lucy been so relieved to hear Walden's deep, soothing tones. She reached for the phone but the nurse held it away from her. "Do you work with a Lucy Guardino?"

"Yes. She's my boss. Supervisory special agent in charge of our Sexual Assault Felony Enforcement squad. Why?" Concern edged his voice. "Has something happened?"

"Could you please describe her?"

Lucy rolled her eyes. She didn't have time for this nonsense. Walden responded with a thumbnail description of her, enough to satisfy the nurse, who finally handed Lucy the phone. Lucy held it close to her lips, straining to raise her voice loud enough to carry through the airwaves.

"Find Nick and Megan," she said. "And secure my mother—she should be at my house with Megan. Nick's at the VA. This morning I was abducted, and the man threatened my family. He has my administrator database code, so call Taylor and have him run a security sweep of the system and alert Clarksburg and Quantico." Her voice faded to a thin, raspy whisper.

"Are you safe now?" Walden asked.

"Yes." Lucy could barely manage the single syllable.

The nurse interrupted. "She has several fractures and severe damage to her left foot and ankle. The doctors are talking to Three Rivers about a transfer to get her to the surgical specialists she needs to save her leg."

Lucy grabbed the phone back. "Get my family to safety."

"On it," he assured her. "Can you describe any of the subjects?"

"I—" She paused, realizing that the nurse was listening to an admission of guilt. What the hell, it was self-defense, pure and simple. "I killed the man I saw. During my escape. A county deputy, Renfew, ID'd him as Lloyd Cramer. I don't know how many accomplices he has."

"Got it. Let me check on your family and tag this deputy as well as Taylor. I'll call you back soon as I have answers." He hung up.

Lucy sagged back in the chair, still gripping the phone like it was a lifeline. "One more call?" she asked the nurse in a meek tone. "My husband. Please?"

Walden had suitably impressed the nurse, who nodded. "Of course. No problem. I'm going to see if they're transferring you or not. Agent Guardino." She added the last in a tone of respect.

Lucy couldn't care less about the title or her medical care. All she cared about was reaching Nick. She called his cell, holding her breath until he answered. "Callahan here."

She couldn't respond right away: her heart felt as if it had leapt into her throat, swelling with gratitude. Nick was alive. He was okay.

"Hello?" he repeated, his Virginia accent leaking through. "Anybody there?"

"It's me," she said. "Lucy," she added, in case her hoarse whisper wasn't clear.

"Lucy, what's wrong?"

"Where's Megan? Have you seen or spoken with her or my mom?"

"There's a story." Country-western music in the background. He was in his car—the only place he listened to that radio station. "She conned your mother into letting her and Emma get a ride after karate from Emma's older sister. Only instead of going to Emma's house, they went to check on Zeke at the vet's. And then Emma and her sister left Megan there while they went to that damn movie."

Megan was alone? Panic parched her mouth. Before she was able to form any words, Nick continued, "Just picked up the little rug rat and we're on our way home to have dinner with your mom. Say hi, Megan. It will be the last time you get to use a phone for a long, long time."

"Mom." Megan's voice carried through, lighting Lucy's heart with a joyous fire. "Tell Dad he's overreacting. I didn't mean to lie, not really. But I knew you didn't want me going to the movie, and I really, really wanted to see Zeke, make sure he was okay. And I asked Grams for permission—well, kind of—so there's no reason to ground me."

"We'll see about that," Nick said. "Anyway, what's up? Your voice sounds funny—don't tell me you got into a shouting match with those bozos in Harrisburg. Hey, Walden's on the other line."

Lucy chose her words carefully, not sure if Megan could hear her. "Nick. Don't go home. I never made it to Harrisburg. A man threatened me as well as my family—"

"Are you okay?" His voice changed, became razor sharp.

"I'm fine. I had a little accident. They brought me to Riverside Community."

"We're on our way. What about your mother? She's waiting at the house."

"Walden's sending someone. He'll arrange an escort for you as well."

"Why? Thanks to Megan's escapades, no one could possibly know where we are, and if you're safe at the hospital, then we will be as well. I'll call Walden back, tell him to have your mom brought there."

Great. Just what she didn't need: explaining the events of the day to her mother. But he was right. There was no way her captor's accomplices could know where she was—hell, they probably didn't even know he was dead yet. With her family safe and Walden on the job, she could finally relax.

She glanced at her mangled leg. Thought about the kind of person who would turn a beautiful animal into a vicious killing machine. Decided he'd gotten what he deserved back in that barn. "Is Megan's puppy okay?"

Nick's laughter was better than any pain medicine the doctors had. "You big softy. Yes, he's fine. The vet said we can bring him home tomorrow."

Exhaustion washed over her, pulling her under like a riptide. "Okay. Good. I'll see you soon."

"Love you, Lucy-loo," he whispered before hanging up.

"Love you, too," she replied, even though the line had already gone dead.

THEN
3:53 P.M.

Her scream died, burying Nick's name in silence. Dear Lord, what had she done?

Sobs shook her—real tears beyond her control. Nick would be okay, she promised herself. He could take care of himself, he was safe at the VA, he'd be all right.

Lies to dull the real pain.

The man grunted in satisfaction, made a show of sending a text on his phone before pocketing it, then circled behind her, embracing her once more, his lips close to her ear as he whispered, "Nick it is."

He slid the rope that circled her chest out from under her arms, transforming it into a noose around her neck. "Get up, Lucy. Your work isn't done."

The noose suspended from the overhead eyehooks was just tight enough to remind her how easy it would be to die: all she had to do was lean her weight forward. A few minutes later, it would all be over. If he hurt her family, she might consider that option. But only as a last resort—she wasn't giving up the fight. Not yet.

"What more do you want?" she asked from her position sitting on the floor.

Instead of answering, he pulled her to her feet and lifted her back up onto the cinder block. Gone was the gentleness he'd shown when he lowered her into the pit earlier. Now he handled her as if she were less than human, an inconvenient object to be dealt with.

She fought to find her balance on the cinder block. Keeping her good foot planted and allowing her injured one to dangle was almost as painful as bracing both feet on the narrow square. Suddenly the rope around her neck yanked taut. Her body jerked up, handcuffed arms arcing behind her.

The cinder block wobbled beneath her, her foot slipped, and the noose tightened, digging into her neck. She gasped for air, could barely make a sound.

"Whoops, not yet," he muttered. He repositioned her foot on the cinder block, then dug a finger between the rope and her skin, loosening it enough that she could breathe.

Lucy blinked against the wave of anxiety that swamped her as she hauled in one lungful of air after another, hyperventilating, rejoicing in the simple act of breathing.

"Okay then," he said in a calm tone that made her wish for just one chance to wrap her hands around his throat as tight as the noose he'd forced on her. "Guess I'll be going."

He used a corner of the cinder block to boost himself up to the opening above them, almost knocking Lucy off-balance once more. The noose tightened, but not enough to cut off her air. She fought to regain her footing on the block as he swung free of the pit.

To her surprise, he didn't close the lid immediately. A few minutes after he left, water gushed from one of the pipes, flowing so hard and fast its spray quickly soaked her.

"What are you doing?" she shouted into the rapidly growing darkness, straining to be heard. "I gave you what you wanted!"

His laughter echoed from above, waning sunlight shimmering blood-red from the water filling the tank. Then he appeared once more. "I'm going to check out the code you gave me. If you told me the truth, I won't be back. The Mexicans will have to be happy watching you either drown or hang yourself.

"But," he turned the simple word into a dire warning, "if you've tried to double-cross me, then I will return. Before the tank fills. And I'll bring your daughter with me. You might want to stick around for that—if you lied and I get back and you've killed yourself, I'm giving her to the Mexicans."

"No. You said I could choose. Leave Megan alone. I told you the truth. The code

119

works. I promise." The rope around her neck made it hard to scream loud enough for her voice to carry above the sound of the rushing water. Not to mention the pain shooting through her as she struggled to keep her balance with the water surging against the cinder block. It took all her will power and concentration to keep enough of her weight on the block to prevent the water from pushing it away.

"I sure hope so, Lucy. For Megan's sake. But either way, Nick dies. Like I said. I'm a man of my word." He slid the lid closed, leaving her alone in the black emptiness of the tank.

Lucy didn't waste time or energy. She focused her entire being into moving her handcuffed hands into the jacket pocket where Megan's bracelet lay. On that and not losing her footing on the damn cinder block. Hard to do between the gushing water below and her entire body suspended from the noose, shaking above.

Finally, her fingers grasped the bracelet. She twisted the Paracord until she had a firm grip on the handcuff key concealed in the clasp. She had to bend her wrist and contort her arms to get the key into the lock.

Just as she flexed her wrists far enough to turn the key, the cinder block wobbled an inch too far and toppled, leaving her body dangling from the noose. The rope cut into the flesh around her neck, cutting off her air. She kept working the key; it was her only hope.

Her entire weight pulled against the noose that strangled her. Her vision flared red against the blackness surrounding her. But she managed to keep control of her fingers long enough to turn the key. The click she'd been waiting for resonated through her entire body.

She fumbled one hand free and pried her fingers beneath the rope strangling her. Gasping for air, each breath burning her throat, she clung to the rope. Without the cinder block, she'd have to use the rope and the wall for leverage—not easy with one leg out of commission, but it was the only way.

Lucy gritted her teeth and pushed her leg against the wall to lift her weight enough so she could pull the rope loose and free her head from the noose. Then she dropped to the floor, landing on her good foot and hanging onto the rope with one hand. Using the other to find the cinder block and set it back upright, she took a deep breath and gathered her strength for the climb out.

The water was already up to her ankles, but that was the least of her worries. If he was monitoring the camera—she assumed it was positioned in the other pipe, the one that didn't have water flowing through it—then this might be an even shorter escape than her earlier one.

And the dog? What if the dog was waiting up there for her?

She grabbed the rope and pulled up her good leg to stand on the cinder block. Dog or no dog, killer or no killer, she was Nick's only hope.

She'd be damned if she'd let anything stop her from saving him and Megan.

CHAPTER 11

THE NURSE RETURNED just as Lucy was wiping her tears of relief with the sleeve of her gown. "Everything okay?"

Lucy sniffed and smiled. "Yes. My family's safe. They're on their way."

"Great." The nurse pushed Lucy's chair back into the trauma bay. She grabbed a warm blanket from a steel cabinet and tucked it around Lucy's lap. She didn't ask for the cell phone back; Lucy hung onto it, hoping that Nick or Walden would call and update her.

"Let's get a move on," the waiting doctor said.

"Where?" Lucy asked.

"The surgeons at Three Rivers want an MRI.

123

We only have one tech this time of night, but I told them this is a priority." The doctor barely made eye contact as he spoke, standing over Lucy and looking down on her. It made her neck hurt to look up at him, so Lucy didn't bother.

"I'm not leaving until my family gets here."

"We'll send the scan to Three Rivers by computer. They'll decide whether or not to LifeFlight you." He spoke as if what she wanted were irrelevant.

"My family can drive me. Silly to waste a helicopter trip." Lucy wasn't arguing just to be a contrarian, although she definitely enjoyed pissing off the arrogant doctor. Driving this time of night—especially with Walden escorting them— would only take ten or fifteen minutes longer than flying.

The main reason was that Nick and Megan couldn't come with her on a helicopter. And once she had them here, safely in her arms, there was no way in hell she was letting them go again. Or her mother.

She picked up the cell phone the nurse had lent her. Better warn Mom that the police were stopping by the house and Walden was coming to pick her up. Mom liked Walden, but she did not like being ordered around or rushed. Thankfully, Walden was less likely to annoy her than Lucy would have if she'd been able to go herself.

"The tech's doing a CAT scan now," the doctor said to the nurse. "Can you get her down to MRI and prep her?" His tone made it clear that he was past ready to get this difficult patient out of his ER and into the hands of someone else.

"No problem."

Lucy dialed her mom's cell. No answer. Probably didn't even have it with her. She left a message on the voice mail just in case.

The nurse pushed her toward the hall. The deputy waited there, looking a bit abashed—he'd spoken with Walden, no doubt. Lucy met his gaze, held her wrists up to ask if he was going to use handcuffs, and he shook his head and turned to lead them through the ER, hand on the butt of his gun as if expecting an ambush from the snotty-nosed kids slumped in chairs in the waiting room or the old man wheezing as he pushed an IV pole down the hall.

Lucy tried her home phone. No answer. Maybe the police had escorted her mom out of the residence while they cleared it and checked for danger? A thin hum of anxiety vibrated through her. Her captor had said he was going after Nick. Mom should have been safe at Lucy's house.

If her captor was a man of his word.

"We're shorthanded," the nurse prattled as they rolled down the corridor. "Flu and RSV hitting hard, not to mention that stomach bug. I think the radiology tech is doing a belly CT, but hopefully we won't have to wait too long." They reached an elevator bank, where several visitors stood waiting.

Lucy barely saw them as she stabbed the phone, calling Walden this time.

The deputy commandeered the first elevator that arrived and shooed the visitors away. "What floor?"

"Basement," the nurse answered. "The MRI's one of the older ones. Only thing down there. Except the morgue."

Idiot, Lucy berated herself as she waited for Walden to pick up. What the hell had she been thinking? Believing for an instant that the psycho who'd taken and tortured her would ever keep his word? Fear and guilt collided. Walden finally answered but was cut off almost immediately as the call was dropped.

"You won't get any reception," the nurse said, sliding the phone from Lucy's hand and pocketing it. "Can't have it near the MRI battery, anyway."

The elevator doors opened and they entered a dimly lit hall. It smelled less hospital and more moldy basement. The tiny squeak from the chair's wheels on the dingy linoleum echoed and bounced from the exposed pipes overhead. The walls were cinder block, painted an institutional pale green meant to be calming but that reminded Lucy of baby puke.

Which made her think of Megan. Wished she'd had time to talk to her. But they'd be here soon—it was only a fifteen-minute drive.

But what about Mom? "Is there another phone I can use?" she asked the nurse. "I really need to check in with my family."

They reached the far end of the corridor, where the MRI suite was. The deputy opened the door to a waiting area, took a look inside, saw the room was empty, held the door as the nurse pushed Lucy inside, then closed the door to stand guard outside.

A row of chairs stood along the near wall. The far wall had several curtained changing areas. A reception desk, empty except for a phone and a computer terminal, guarded a large solid door leading to the MRI examination area. On the wall behind the desk was an emergency call button with a small intercom speaker.

"You can use the phone as soon as we get you prepped," the nurse told her.

"How long will this take?"

"Thirty-forty minutes." The nurse scrutinized the bag of IV fluid hanging from the pole extending up from the back of the chair. "All done. That's your first dose of antibiotic." With swift fingers, she detached the tubing from the IV, leaving Lucy's hands free. "Your vitals have been fine, and they have a special monitor of their own." She removed the sticky monitor leads from Lucy's chest and unhooked her from the portable monitor that hung from the back of the chair.

"Okay, now I need you to answer this questionnaire." She took a clipboard from a hook on the wall. "You work on that while I go check on the tech." She nodded to the large red-and-white sign on the opposite wall, warning about the MRI's powerful magnet. "Don't skip any questions. We don't want any surprises. I once had a patient who forgot about a dental bridge—not a pretty sight."

Lucy nodded and took the pen she offered. The nurse left, and Lucy began the slow process of wheeling the chair with her one good hand, ignoring the questionnaire, to head to the desk where the phone was. To her surprise, the deputy entered and moved to stand in front of her, thumbs hooked into his duty belt, fingers stretched along the wide belt buckle.

"You know officer safety comes first," he said. His way of apologizing.

"Of course," she answered. He'd done everything by the book. Wasn't anyone's fault that the book didn't cover situations like this.

"And after finding Lloyd like that . . ." His voice trailed off. "You sure he's the one did this to you? Sure doesn't sound like him. No history of violence. Bit of a prepper type, keeps to himself, except for his dogs of course. Trains them and rents them out as guard dogs. Loves those animals more than most humans."

A sudden thought speared through Lucy, distracting her from her mission to get to the phone. No. She couldn't have—but the barn had been dark, she'd never gotten a good look at man's face, just the faintest impression as they'd struggled. "Photo?"

"Of Lloyd Cramer?" He pulled a driver's license encased in an evidence bag from his pocket, held it in front of her. "This is him."

Brown hair. Brown eyes. Lucy hunched over the photo, studying it for clues, her stomach revolting as her fingers gripped the plastic bag so tight it almost slipped through them. This was not her man—not the man who'd kidnapped her.

The man was still out there. Her family was

still in danger.

She'd killed the wrong man.

CHAPTER 12

FOR A LONG moment, the only sound in the room was the buzz and crackle of the fluorescent lights. Lucy tried to gather her thoughts. Had she killed an innocent man? No, he had a gun, had attacked her . . . Farmers carry guns. She was on his land, hiding in the dark . . . No, the dog was his. He had to be working with the man who'd taken her.

The man who was still out there. Her family wasn't safe yet.

The phone on the desk rang, the shrill noise jump-starting Lucy's attention. She thrust her fear aside as the deputy answered. "Yeah, she's right

131

here." He wheeled her to the desk and handed her the receiver. "It's Special Agent Walden."

Walden. The man had impeccable timing. "There's definitely one subject still out there," she said. "Where are you?"

"I'm on my way to Riverside." His voice sounded distant, heavy.

"Is my mother with you?"

A pause. "Lucy, I need you to wait at the hospital. Don't leave until I get there."

"Why? What happened?" Fear clenched her heart so tight she couldn't breathe. "Are Nick and Megan okay?" Then she realized he hadn't answered her original question. "Walden, let me speak to my mom."

"I can't. Lucy—"

She knew that tone. Had used it herself when preparing victims for bad news. The worst possible kind of news. "No. No, it can't be. He said—"

The man had said he'd go after one of her family. A man of his word.

Suddenly the deputy and everything else in the room seemed very far away as Lucy's world collapsed. Not her mother . . . Denial, always the first instinct. No protection against the truth revealed by Walden's silence.

Finally, Lucy found her voice again. "What happened?"

"The locals I sent to your house found her. She's on her way to Three Rivers."

Relief rushed over her. "She's alive. What did he do to her?"

Bastard must have gone straight to her home after leaving Lucy in the pit. Maybe seven o'clock wasn't a deadline but the time when his window of opportunity opened. Her mind picked at the tiny details, refusing to recognize the gruesome truth. Her mother injured, her home a crime scene . . . and all of it her fault.

Lucy closed her eyes, tried to see her mother's face. She couldn't. Her entire body was awash in cold, more numb than it had been when she climbed from the pit into the snow. She swallowed twice before she could force any words out. "How bad?"

He hesitated, and she knew it was worse than she'd dared think.

"Don't make me imagine it, Walden."

They both knew the things Lucy had seen in the course of her work. The stuff of nightmares. The truth could only be a tonic to whatever horrors her fear and imagination could conjure.

"A knife," Walden finally said. "He used a knife."

Christ. The phone slipped from Lucy's grasp. She fumbled for it on her lap.

"She was unconscious but still had a pulse," Walden continued. "But the medics—"

"She's not going to die." In Lucy's head the words translated to an anguished plea: she *couldn't* die. Not her mother. Not because of Lucy.

"Nick? Megan?" Lucy asked, both hands awkwardly gripping the phone. *Please, God . . .* She couldn't finish the silent prayer, too fearful it might not be answered.

133

"Just got off the phone with Nick. They were pulling into the Riverside parking lot. I told him to find you and stay there. I'm only a few minutes out, and the county is sending more men as well. I was just calling to make sure you were still there. I'll alert hospital security as soon as I hang up."

His voice, calmly delineating the mundane tasks associated with protecting her and her family, helped to keep her focused. It didn't stop the roiling in her gut or the chills that had suddenly overtaken her, but if Nick and Megan were safe, nothing else mattered. Except . . . Mom . . . No, she still couldn't quite make that fact feel real. Her mother. She clutched at the blanket over her chest with the fingers of her left hand, twisting it into a tight ball wedged against her splint. Not Mom. No. She was going to be all right. She had to be.

A knock came at the door, and the deputy answered. Nick and Megan?

"Talk later," she mumbled into the phone, then hung up. With her good hand, she turned the wheelchair around to face the door. Saw the deputy standing, relaxed. Couldn't see who he was speaking to but heard the words "FBI."

The deputy backed up, holding the door open for the people outside. Lucy straightened, anxious to see Nick and Megan but also haunted by the bad news she'd have to share with them.

The door clicked shut, and the deputy turned to her, leaving his back to the newcomer. A man in a conservative dark suit. Brown hair, brown eyes. Six feet. Caucasian.

Her captor.

Lucy's warning emerged in a rasp, too late to help. The gunshot was a mere muffled pop that would never make it past the thick walls of the MRI suite. The deputy's eyes went wide, then he slumped to the ground, a gaping bloody hole in the base of his skull.

"Nice to see you again, Lucy." The man stepped over the deputy's corpse. "Well, maybe not for you."

He glanced at his watch. "Good thing I was just down the road at the technical college. Remember the campus safety initiative you spearheaded? Hooking up all the local colleges with the NCIC and the Uniform Crime Reporting databases so serial rapists could be identified and caught sooner? Can't tell you how helpful the folks over there were. So ready to help an FBI agent chasing a sexual predator."

He slid a black leather wallet from his pocket and flipped it open like an actor on TV. Lucy's stolen credentials. He'd been following a timetable, not a deadline. Seven p.m. Perfect time to find a small campus security office understaffed as the long twelve-hour night shift arrived.

She had given him what he wanted, leaving him enough time to visit her home and find her mother first. Anger tunneled her vision, and she forced herself to breathe deep, clear it. She needed to find a way to stop him. Now.

Nick and Megan are on their way. The words hammered through her mind. One way or the other, the man couldn't be here when they arrived. Her heart pounded at the thought of what "the other" option might entail.

What choice did she have? Trapped in a wheelchair. No way could she reach the phone or emergency call button behind her before he struck. Anyway, did she really want to call civilians here, risk their lives? Bad enough her own mother had been hurt because of her.

"Why are you here?" she asked, hoping his answer might provide her a way out of this.

He smiled. That same half-joking, half-leering smile he'd given her out in the field after he'd sicced the dog on her. "You saw my face. Can't have you live to tell anyone. Besides, I promised you that you would die today." He flashed a wink at her. "I'm a man of my word."

She had a hard time finding enough spit to swallow. Gave up and simply nodded. Sat up straight and tall in the chair. She needed this to happen now, before Nick and Megan arrived. "Get it over with."

His smile widened, but he didn't shoot. Instead, he lowered his weapon and kicked the guard's body to the wall behind the door. "Don't you want to say good-bye to your family first?"

He opened the door and gestured outside. "You can come in now."

Lucy's blood turned to ice, horror freezing her from the inside out as Megan rushed in, followed by Nick.

CHAPTER 13

MEGAN ONLY HAD eyes for her mom as she raced through the room, falling into a half crouch beside the chair to hug Lucy fiercely. "Mom, are you okay? What happened?"

Lucy didn't answer; she just held on, wrapping her arms around Megan—splint be damned—as if she could stop any bullets aimed at her daughter. But it was Nick she was worried about.

After fifteen years of marriage, some of her

habits had rubbed off on him. Including how she entered a room. Just as she would have, Nick paused, assessing the situation in two blinks. Cataloguing her injuries. Catching the warning in her eyes. Seeing the dead deputy half-hidden behind the open door.

He was torn between running inside to protect her and Megan, fleeing to get them help, and attacking the man behind him. The tug-of-war ended with Nick awkwardly pivoting, fist raised, only to be met by a pistol in his face.

The man chuckled, jerked his chin to invite Nick all the way inside, then closed the door and locked it. "Figured you'd want a little privacy for our family reunion."

"Who are you?" Nick asked. There was a dangerous edge to his voice and his fists were still clenched. Lucy saw his struggle as he forced his emotions aside and tried to negotiate. "What do you want?"

The man was having none of it. He glanced past Nick to Lucy. "Does he really think I'm going to fall for any of his shrink BS?"

"He doesn't know you like I do," she answered. Her voice was getting stronger—driven by desperation or simply a sign that the swelling was beginning to ease, she wasn't sure. Good thing, though, because her voice and her knowledge of this man were their only weapons.

"Guess we'll have to change that." Before Lucy could protest, the man raised his pistol. For a heartbeat she thought he was going to shoot Nick like he had the deputy, but at the last minute, the man instead struck him on the side of the head with a blow so forceful Nick fell to the floor. Then he kicked Nick in his stomach.

"Dad!" Megan screamed, but Lucy held her tight, forcing her face into Lucy's shoulder.

"Don't look," she whispered.

Nick groaned, doubled up in pain, hands up to protect his head, blood seeping through his fingers.

The man nudged Nick with his shoe. "Getting the picture, doc? Oh, and by the way, your taste in music sucks. How can you listen to that wailing and whining country crap?"

Another piece of the puzzle. The man couldn't track Nick or Megan by their phones— they both had units secured by FBI software. He must have placed a tracker and bug inside Nick's car.

Lucy squeezed Megan tighter. She ran her fingers through Megan's hair and rubbed her shoulder, brushing the IV pole on the back of the chair. She remembered how the nurse had placed the metal rod into its housing, tightening it with a simple collar screw. Hope flared through Lucy as she stretched her fingers to try to loosen the screw.

Megan placed a hand over hers. "He'll see. Let me." She breathed the words into Lucy's ear.

"Everything's going to be okay, Megan," Lucy said, patting Megan's back. "Now, get behind me."

Megan obeyed, moving to crouch behind Lucy's chair. The man shook his head at them.

"Shouldn't make promises you can't keep, Lucy."

She didn't. Not ever. "Let them go. The police are on their way."

"You telling me what to do?" The silence between them filled with hostility. She had one chance to play this right—play him right—and save her family.

"No. Of course not. I'm giving you information. You're a smart man. Leave now and you can slip away. The police will never find you."

"You know this is all your fault, right?" he said. "You chose this path. From the moment you decided you were better than the rest of us, that you were a hero."

The vision of the man she'd killed filled her mind. "I'm no hero."

"No. You're not. It's time your family knew that." He pulled out his phone. "I'm going to play our conversation for Nick and Megan. Let Nick hear how you chose him to die. How you sent me to kill him."

She remained silent, knowing anything she said would make it worse. Nick would understand.

"And Megan. How about if I show her what I did to your mother? What *you* let happen, Lucy. After you disobeyed me and went after my man. Actions have consequences, Lucy."

"Grams?" Megan said, her voice a strange combination of fury and worry. "Don't you dare hurt my grandmother!"

"Poor girl," he said. "If she lives through the night, she's going to need some serious counseling. Oh, that reminds me, you really should keep your knives sharpened. They were so dull. Caused much more pain than necessary—something else you're to blame for."

Lucy bit the inside of her cheek to avoid screaming in frustration. "You're right. It's all my fault. You're angry. At me."

"Trying to manipulate me again, Lucy? You know that won't work. I'm in control here. I've always been in control. I'm the one with the power."

"I know that. How could I not? You hold my family's lives in your hands." She couldn't risk glancing down at Nick, had to keep the killer's gaze locked on her, but in the edge of her peripheral vision she saw Nick slowly stretch his body. Preparing to strike. "If you wait for the police, no one will get out alive."

"Including your family." His gaze dared her to say the words, make them fact.

"Including my family."

What was Megan doing back there? It shouldn't take this long to loosen the screw. She still wasn't sure how Megan would get the IV pole to Lucy when the time was right. Timing. It all depended on split-second timing.

"Everyone you love will die because of you, Lucy. Because you thought you were smarter, better than me. Because you dared to think you could win."

"But I'm not. Not smarter, not better, not going to win. We both know that. And you can prove it. Take control of the situation. Leave now

141

before the police get here." Her words came through clenched jaws. She held her breath, hoping he didn't see the flaw in her argument—it would only take a few seconds for him to kill Nick and Megan before escaping. But she was counting on his need to see their pain—her pain. To see her crushed, totally surrendering.

To emerge the victor.

She almost had him when a pounding sounded on the door. "Open up. FBI!"

The man whirled in anger, aiming his weapon first at Nick, then at Megan, who ducked down behind Lucy. Lucy pushed herself out of the chair and stood, blocking the man's line of fire. From the corner of her eye, she saw that the light on the intercom beside Megan was now blinking red. Ahh . . . smart girl.

The man said nothing, but his gaze filled with venom. He placed a foot on Nick's throat and aimed once more at him. Then he cocked one eyebrow, daring Lucy to make a move. She stood, unsteady, weight on one foot.

Lucy ended the silence, unable to bear it anymore. "Take me hostage. Leave them."

She had to get him out of here before he realized there was no escape. Given the basement's layout, stepping out into the hall would be stepping into what SWAT guys called the fatal funnel. "You don't have much time. They won't negotiate for long."

"No. I don't have much time." His tone had changed. Less rushed. Lower, restrained . . . in control. Shit. He'd made a decision, and it wasn't the one she wanted. "Neither do you. We'll finish this. Now. Together."

CHAPTER 14

"WHO DIES FIRST?" the man asked. Only a few feet separated him from Lucy but the way she was tottering, pain spiking through her leg, she knew she'd never reach him. Not in time. "Your choice, Lucy."

Nick looked up from his position on the floor. Met her eyes. Smiled. Then scissored his legs to kick the man's feet out from under him. The gun went off, a bullet striking one of the chairs against the far wall. The man landed on one knee, aiming at Nick.

A blur of motion came from beside Lucy as Megan slid the IV pole free. She ran forward, using it like one of her karate staffs, darting to strike the man's wrist, then whipping the pole back, swinging it into the man's face. The man dropped the gun. Nick scrambled to grab it.

Nick leapt to his feet, holding the pistol, hauling Megan back as she aimed yet another blow on the downed man. Megan's hair had fallen into her face, and when she brushed it back, her expression was fury personified.

Lucy hadn't moved. "Megan, get behind me," she ordered. Nick gave Megan a quick hug, and Megan backed up a few steps, standing between Lucy and the man on the ground and still holding the pole like a club.

The door burst open, and Walden rushed inside, accompanied by a sheriff's deputy. The deputy whirled on Nick, but Walden stopped him. "He's one of ours."

The deputy knelt to secure the man whose eye was already swollen shut and wrist bent at an unnatural angle. Megan was stronger than she looked—but Lucy knew that already.

Lucy reached for Megan, who was trembling from head to toe. Hugged her hard from behind. "Nick, take her out of here."

He gave the weapon to Walden, hauled in a breath, eyes wide, as he turned to Lucy. But he wrapped an arm around Megan, carefully steering her around the fallen deputy and as far away as possible from the man on the floor.

"Walden—" She didn't have to say anything more. He nodded and joined Nick and Megan, escorting them out of the room.

"I made a mistake," the man on the floor said, his voice muffled as the deputy pushed his head down to search him.

"You made a huge mistake," Lucy agreed, most of her mind mentally mapping Nick and Megan's exit to safety. Adrenaline jangled her nerves. All she could see was the man's gun aimed at Nick, then at Megan as Megan swung the pole. A split second either way . . . She turned her head away, swallowing hard against acid that filled her throat as her gut clenched with fear. She'd almost lost them.

"I chose the wrong victim," the man said. Why the hell wouldn't he just shut up?

"You chose the wrong family." She sank down into the wheelchair, hoping he didn't see that she simply didn't have any strength left to stand. She wished the deputy would hurry and take this filth from her sight so she could get out of here and be with Nick and Megan. She still had to tell them about her mother. Needed to find out if her mother was okay.

Exhaustion tempted her. Her eyes were so heavy, her energy gone. She kicked her bad leg against the chair, using the pain to keep her alert. Couldn't relax. Not until she made it to Three Rivers and her mom.

"*Your* family. They don't make you vulnerable or weak." He craned his head up to meet her gaze.

147

God, she was tired. So very tired. She didn't have patience for his games. "No. They don't. They give me strength."

"They're why you never lost hope. Why I couldn't break you."

He had. Deep inside, she knew he had. She wasn't sure if that fracture could ever be healed. But she wouldn't give him the satisfaction of knowing. The deputy hauled him to his feet as she said, "No. You couldn't."

A security guard appeared in the doorway, holding a pistol. He holstered it and joined the deputy to remove the man. The man acted as if they weren't there, as if no one existed except him and Lucy. He twisted within his captors' grips to look over his shoulder at her. Then he smiled. "Thanks for the fun, Lucy. You were the best ever."

Startled, she glanced up at his words. His expression wasn't of a man defeated. Rather of a man who'd just won, big-time.

As the two men escorting him separated to fit their threesome through the door, the killer abruptly dropped his weight, pivoted to push the deputy away, and grabbed the security guard's weapon with his restrained hands. Then he vanished into the hallway.

Where Nick and Megan were. Terror propelled Lucy back onto her feet as the two men raced after him, leaving her hobbling behind. The sound of gunshots…Oh God, oh God . . .

"Nick! Megan!" she screamed, but the gunfire drowned her out.

Finally, there was silence. Somehow she'd made it to the doorway, but now she wasn't sure if she could bear to see what was on the other side. She lurched into the hallway.

The security guard was down, the deputy standing over him. Beyond them the man in the suit sat slumped, back against the wall, his white shirt now peppered with blood. More blood gushed from his mouth, and his face was slack, eyes dull. He still gripped the stolen pistol, held awkwardly to one side of his body in his handcuffed hands.

Walden approached him, weapon drawn. He kicked away the man's pistol and checked his pulse. "He's gone."

The dead man had chosen his own way out, kept control of his destiny, just like he said he would.

She couldn't see Nick or Megan. Had he destroyed what was left of her family during his suicide-by-cop?

Using the wall for support, she limped down the hall.

"Nick? Megan?" She could barely say their names. Her heart was already shredded, caught between hope and despair. She couldn't tear her gaze away from the dead man. The man with all the answers.

She spotted movement at the end of the hallway. A door opening. Nick and Megan. Running toward her. Safe and whole and alive.

The pain in her foot vanished as she lunged forward, pulling them into her arms.

She had no idea how much time passed before the medical people arrived. "Guess I'll get that MRI at Three Rivers," the nurse said. Lucy's gaze caught on the dead man, now surrounded by police officers.

She didn't even know his name. She didn't care.

Just as Nick was helping her back into the wheelchair, Walden reappeared, clenching his phone in his hand. He met her eyes, shaking his head sorrowfully.

A howl of anguish escaped her as Lucy realized the price she'd paid for surviving.

EPILOGUE

"DO YOU UNDERSTAND what I've explained to you about the complications of the procedure, Mrs. Guardino?" The vascular surgeon at Three Rivers Medical Center wielded a clipboard filled with consent forms. "Animal maulings aren't like normal injuries. We're dealing with nerve damage, crush injuries, infection, necrotic tissue. There's a good chance we won't be able to save the leg. And, even if we do, it's questionable how much function you'll regain."

Nick watched as Lucy stared listlessly at the

151

forms. She wore a patient gown as well as an assortment of bandages, splints, and dressings. She lay on a stretcher, and her left leg was propped up on a foam triangle, strapped into place, a thin layer of gauze hiding the ugly mass of swollen and dead tissue. IV tubing bristled from her right shoulder, where they'd inserted a special line that fed into her heart to give her fluids and antibiotics. Medication that was probably too late to save her foot, but that could still save her life.

She finally answered the surgeon. "You're saying I won't be taking my husband dancing." Then she laughed. A hollow sound, it thudded against the tile walls and made the seasoned trauma doctor flinch.

Nick didn't blame him. Ever since Walden had told them about Lucy's mother dying, it was as if his vibrant wife who never surrendered to anything had been lost to pain and exhaustion and grief. Not to mention the haze of drugs.

At least he hoped he could blame the drugs for most of it. They'd wear off in time. The rest...

She signed the form the surgeon held for her, her signature a random scribble, not at all her usual confident loops and spirals.

Nick couldn't help but wonder if Lucy would ever be herself again. A flutter of fear beat against his chest wall as he held his wife's hand and she didn't return his loving grasp.

Back at the other hospital, he'd been torn between leaving Megan with Walden and staying with Lucy. It was the type of decision Lucy made every day, but he'd felt lost, overwhelmed. Until

Walden rescued him by declaring the case a matter of national security, thus federal jurisdiction, and bringing both Nick and Megan here to Three Rivers to be with Lucy.

Only Lucy wasn't here. Not really. Sometime after that man had died, after she'd seen her daughter forced to defend them all, Lucy—*his* Lucy, the fierce warrior filled with passion and compassion—she'd vanished, leaving only this empty shell of a woman.

The surgeon also seemed to realize Lucy wasn't herself, even though he'd only met her a few hours ago. He turned his clipboard toward Nick. "Perhaps you should give consent as well, Mr. Guardino."

"It's Callahan," Nick corrected. "Dr. Callahan, in fact." He sounded like an ass, saying that, didn't know why he did, except he desperately needed to regain some control over this nightmare, over his life.

"Oh, you're a medical doctor?"

Nick took the clipboard and pen. "No. PhD. Psychology." He scrawled his name. Signing consent for the surgeon to cut off part of his wife's body.

The forms completed, the surgeon lost interest. "A nurse will be in to take her to the OR in a few minutes." He left them.

Nick had never felt more alone. Standing beside his wife, holding her limp hand, waiting for this all to be over. Would it ever be over?

During their fifteen years of marriage, he'd seen Lucy through every possible emotional storm: passion about a case, frustration at the system, anger when justice wasn't served. He'd seen her exhausted, in despair, even frightened.

He'd never seen her surrender. Not like this. Vacant, drained. Defeated.

"It's going to be okay," he murmured into her hair as he kissed her forehead, avoiding the staples holding together one of her many lacerations.

No response.

He was thankful the hospital staff hadn't let Megan into the pre-op area. His stomach knotted at the thought of her seeing her mother like this. Hell, he wasn't sure *he* could bear to see Lucy like this.

"Lucy, really. I promise. It will be okay." He squeezed her hand again, his wedding band rubbing against the empty spot where hers should be. Would they ever get it back? Or would it be forever entombed in the bowels of some evidence locker? "You know me. I never make a promise I can't keep."

He squeezed harder. So hard it had to be painful. She didn't answer, didn't meet his gaze.

The nurse came. "It's time. You can wait in the family area outside the OR."

"No. I'll go with you as far as I can." Nick couldn't bear letting go of Lucy, not one instant before he had to. Together they rolled her stretcher down the hall until they came to a set of double doors leading into the operating suite.

"I'm sorry," the nurse said. "This is as far as you can go. You need to say good-bye now."

Nick reached across Lucy's body to embrace her, his tears wetting her cheeks as he kissed her. Her lips were cold, her face slack.

"I'll be right here," he promised. "Both Megan and I will be here when you wake up."

She blinked at Megan's name. Finally nodded. Squeezed his hand. "Remember what you promised," she whispered, her voice low, so low he could barely make out her words. "Don't forget."

He kissed her again, hope rekindled by the tiny spark that had returned to her. "I won't. It will all be okay. I know it will. You're strong, Lucy. The strongest person I know. You'll make it through this—*we'll* make it through this. I promise."

Her eyes slid closed as if she were too weary to keep them open. But she nodded again. "I believe you. I love you, Nick. And Megan. More than anything."

"I know. We know." He gave her hand one final squeeze as the nurse opened the door and pushed her through to the other side, to the sterile area where ordinary men like Nick were forbidden.

Suddenly it occurred to him that their entire marriage had been like that. Lucy crossing each day into a strange world filled with violence and evil and chaos. A world ordinary people lived their ordinary lives hoping they never had to acknowledge even existed—along with their need for people like Lucy. Men and women strong enough to enter that world and save them.

Now it was Nick's turn to save Lucy—and Megan as well. His entire family was at risk, contaminated by the evil that had escaped from Lucy's world into theirs.

Part of him was angry, wanting to blame Lucy for tonight's bloodshed. If she wasn't the fierce, passionate warrior she was, this would have never happened.

He held onto that pain, using it to fuel the fire he'd need to get through this. Because he'd promised Lucy they would get through this. Because everything that happened to their family was as much his fault as hers.

When he'd first met her, he knew who she was, what she was, and he'd fallen hopelessly in love with her and everything she stood for. Part of him felt a coward that he could never fight on the front lines like she did—part of him felt relieved that because of people like her, he didn't have to.

Nick gripped the railing that ran along the wall, head bowed, fighting to regain some sure footing amid the emotional turmoil engulfing him. Mostly, being with Lucy made him strive to be a better man, to find the courage to change the lives around him just as she did.

When he looked up, Lucy was gone and the doors had closed. He stared at them for a long moment, feeling lost and alone. Then he drew in a deep breath, chasing away ghosts of fear to focus on the one thing he was certain of: Lucy would survive.

With that thought as his anchor, he went in

search of the family area, his mind already spinning with ideas, ways to help both his daughter and wife—and himself. Names of counselors he trusted, victim advocates, child psych specialists, patients he'd worked with, soldiers who would understand what Lucy was going through better than he could...

He was not about to let the darkness claim his family. Never. He'd promised Lucy.

And Nick was a man of his word.

AUTHOR'S NOTE

Dear Readers,

As Lucy says, her family is her greatest strength and what keeps her fighting. You, my readers, are *my* family, and I need you to have faith in Lucy and me.

The story isn't over. Stay tuned for Lucy's return in *Hard Fall*, coming September, 2014.

Thanks for reading!

CJ

ABOUT THE AUTHOR

New York Times and *USA Today* bestselling author of twenty-three novels, former pediatric ER doctor CJ Lyons has lived the life she writes about in her cutting edge Thrillers with Heart.

CJ has been called a "master within the genre" (Pittsburgh Magazine) and her work has been praised as "breathtakingly fast-paced" and "riveting" (Publishers Weekly) with "characters with beating hearts and three dimensions" (Newsday).

Her novels have won the International Thriller Writers' prestigious Thriller Award, the RT Reviewers' Choice Award, the Readers' Choice Award, the RT Seal of Excellence, and the Daphne du Maurier Award for Excellence in Mystery and Suspense.

Learn more about CJ's Thrillers with Heart at www.CJLyons.net

Keep Reading for a Special Sneak Peek of CJ's first book featuring everyone's favorite sociopath teen, Morgan Ames:

FIGHT DIRTY

Coming October, 2014

Chapter 1

The prison guard pressed his palm against Morgan's ass as he waved his wand over her body. She smiled. It wasn't an "Oh baby, so very glad you pulled me aside for this special security screening" smile—although, sheep that he was, he obviously thought so. No, she smiled because she knew that if she wanted, she could kill him.

"You sure you're a lawyer, Ms. Wilson?" he asked, his palm sliding over her hip. The name on her ID was Amy Wilson, twenty-two, residing at 515 Gettysburg Street, Pittsburgh, PA 15206.

Her real name was Morgan Ames. And since her real age was fifteen, she waited, assessing her avenues for escape. The guard's next words would decide if he lived or died.

They were in the administrative section of Rockview State Penitentiary's maximum-security wing. There weren't that many doors between her and freedom. The men guarding them didn't worry her, not as much as the electronically controlled locks. Men she could kill in seconds, but it would take longer to overcome those damn locks.

After she'd passed through the metal detector and had her bag examined, the guard had ushered her to a private screening room. It was small, no windows, walls made of standard construction materials. If she killed him, she'd have to keep it quiet—sound would carry easily through the walls. Beyond them was the reception area where, even though it wasn't quite eight in the morning, women and children waited to be allowed visitation time with their own favorite maximum-security inmate.

The guard, oblivious to his precarious fate, held her breast in his hand as he ran the wand over her outstretched arms. She felt his heat through the silk of her bra and blouse, scented his testosterone rising.

A part of her hoped she'd have to kill him. It was the dangerous side of her, the one she was struggling to control so she didn't end up in a place like this, surrounded by steel bars and razor wire. The part of her that had killed before—and enjoyed it.

"You're much too pretty to be a lawyer."

Her smile didn't waver. His words had just saved his life—although he'd never know it. "I'm just a paralegal. Have to get our client's signature, so we can meet a filing deadline."

"I knew it. Like I said, too pretty—and too nice." He released her and stepped in front of her. "I get off in a few hours—"

The hard part wasn't not killing him, it was not laughing in his face. But Morgan was good at

161

what she did. It's why she could as easily pass for twenty as for twelve. It was all in the attitude and the costume. Match them to your audience's expectations, and no one doubted the rest.

"I'd love to," she said, raising her left hand to grab her leather attaché, letting the overhead light flick against the gold band on her ring finger. A band that was almost a match to the guard's own. "But my husband has plans. You might know him. He's state police, was in the barracks here for a while, Tom Wilson?"

The guard's leer morphed into a grudging nod of respect. Prison guards depended on state troopers for a lot of things, including saving their bacon in the case of a riot. No way in hell would one ever cross a trooper. "Sure, I know Tom. Tell him I say hi."

He yanked the door open and escorted her down the hall to the first of several locked sally ports leading to the secure interview rooms. Idiot never looked back. Despite his uniform and swagger, he was just another sheep, milling about, doing what he was told without thinking. Morgan's smile turned genuine.

The prison corridor was empty except for the two of them and the invisible eyes watching via the cameras positioned overhead. Industrial-grade vinyl flooring and featureless beige walls muted their footsteps. Fluorescent lights flickered above, trying in vain to give the appearance of cheerful sunlight, but the feeble attempt was overwhelmed by the all-consuming stink of sweat and desperation that wept from every surface.

He unlocked the steel door to an interview room. The room was the size of a walk-in closet, no windows except the one in the door, the only furniture a steel table bolted to the floor—a bar running across its top on one side—and two lightweight chairs. There was a bright-red panic button on the wall beside the door and another on the visitor's side of the table. Otherwise the walls were bare.

"He's on his way," the guard said, his tone now surly, as if she'd purposely wasted his time. "You know about Caine, right? He used to take girls like you, held them captive underground in the dark, torturing them, raping them—you name it, he did it." His eyes tightened, holding back his own rapacious fantasies. "He's gonna love you; you're just his type."

With that he left, locking her inside to await the arrival of a serial killer.

Morgan played her role for the overhead camera—video only, audio recordings weren't permitted, a violation of prisoners' rights. Funny world where men like Clinton Caine had rights. That's what happened when you let sheep run things.

She sat down and smoothed out her skirt, a lovely teal and charcoal houndstooth wool-silk blend, bought, not shoplifted, from the South Hills Galleria. Now that she was on her own, Morgan was beyond petty thievery.

She'd just unpacked her folders with the fake

163

legal documents when the door opened. A man's shadow slid into the room even as he remained at the threshold, flanked by two guards, waiting for permission to enter. Permission was granted in the form of one of the guards giving him a shove, forcing him to stumble inside. He wore the orange jumpsuit of a maximum-security prisoner—as if she wouldn't have figured that out from the handcuffs that restrained his wrists behind his back and the shackles around his ankles.

He must have done something to piss them off. Last time she'd visited, a few months ago, they'd had the handcuffs in front so that he could at least walk upright with some semblance of dignity.

For the first time ever, he looked older than his actual fifty-two. His hair was unwashed, uncombed, silver streaks marring the chestnut-brown curls always certain to attract the ladies. His face was pocked with red sores, pustules with ugly yellow crusts. One guard unlocked one of his handcuffs, swiftly bringing his hands to the front where the cuffs were wrapped around the bar running the length of the table and snapped shut again with a click.

The prisoner sat down, his gaze never leaving Morgan. His eyes. They hadn't changed. Two holes burnt into the darkest night sky. Glaring, blazing, yet absolutely indifferent.

Clinton Caine knew what it cost Morgan to come here, to allow herself to be locked inside a cement-block and glass-walled room, trapped behind the razor wire and steel fences surrounding the state penitentiary's maximum-security housing unit. He didn't care. Clint didn't worry about anything except Clint and his ridiculous fantasies of regaining his own freedom.

He remained silent until the guards left and the door closed behind them. Then he leaned forward as if reading the papers she slid across to him. "What'cha bring me, little girl? Better be something worth the cavity search this visit's gonna cost me."

Morgan hid her cringe. His tone was the same one he used when goading fish—his word for the women he kidnapped and killed. A tone that promised no amount of effort would ever be enough to earn a reprieve. His way of reminding her that she existed solely to please him.

He didn't realize that only two things kept him alive: the prison guards monitoring them outside the interview room and Morgan's promise to herself that she'd give up killing.

Good thing, because there was no one she'd rather see dead than this man. Clinton Caine. Her father.

His gaze flicked from the papers to her suit. "Better not be using my hard-earned money for all that fancy crap. This new lawyer is already costing me plenty."

How easily he forgot that while he'd enjoyed himself torturing fish, it was Morgan who had taught herself the skills needed to steal identities and get them money to live on. Didn't matter. To him, it was all his. The world belonged to Clinton

Caine, along with everyone and everything in it.

"If you'd stop firing your lawyers—" she protested.

"That's got nothing to do with you," he snapped. "What I want to hear from you is some good news." He shook his head, mocking her. "You don't call, you don't write. If I didn't know better, I'd think you'd forgotten me, were gonna leave me here to rot."

He reached a hand to take the pen she was holding, caressing her palm intimately, reminding her of what they'd shared. All those women . . . all that blood.

Morgan looked past him, counting the blocks in the concrete wall. Her therapist had taught her to focus on what she wanted long term rather than giving in to her immediate impulses. Delayed gratification. As she counted, imaginary blood sprayed the whitewashed blocks. A pretty arterial spray in the shape of a butterfly.

Wouldn't that be lovely?

"Why did you call me here?" she asked, blinking hard to erase her bloodstained fantasy.

"My smart new lawyer says the same as the other two, that those damn witnesses could sway a jury. Poison them against me." Clint bent closer to her, his breath wafting across the steel table between them, bringing with it the stench of rot and decay.

She pulled her pen from his grasp and tapped the stack of folders before her, redirecting his attention, hiding her disgust.

Masks. Morgan was a pro at slipping masks

on and off at will. Clint didn't even notice the mask she wore now. Not that of a bored paralegal sent to do her boss's dirty work. No. Right now she was concentrating on not jabbing her pen into his jugular.

Veins were better targets than arteries. No muscle in their walls. Hit them, wrench your blade back and forth to shred them, and no amount of pressure would stop the gush of blood that followed.

"You listening to me, girl?" Clint demanded.

Morgan peered through her vision of gorgeous scarlet ribbons flowing from his neck, clashing with the orange prison jumpsuit.

"Sorry," she muttered. Only Clint could make her feel weak or the need to apologize for it. No one else. With the rest of the world she was fearless, relentless, capable of anything.

To Clint she was his little girl, eager to please and obey.

"I said start with those two Feds," he snarled, a spray of saliva accompanying his words. She kept her gaze focused on the table, didn't remind him that he'd gotten caught not by brilliant police work but by his own greed and refusal to curb his sadistic impulses.

"Jenna Galloway and Lucy Guardino." He savored the names of his targets, a smile growing like a cancer on his face. "Start with them, and this will all go away. We can go back to having fun. Just a dad and his baby girl going fishing."

Clint's victims, his fish, they weren't people, not to him—not to Morgan, either. But she was out of the fishing business. For good.

No way in hell was she going to end up trapped in a steel and concrete cage like Clint. Morgan twisted her fingers around her pen until her nails blanched white. No. Way. In. Hell.

It was the reason she'd given up killing. Too risky, even if her last few kills had been bad guys.

The rush of power that came with taking a life, that hadn't changed—in fact, it had gotten stronger, like an addiction, especially when added to the glow of satisfaction when she'd saved Jenna Galloway's life a few months ago. Clint didn't know that little detail. No way was Morgan going to tell him. About how she'd inserted herself into Jenna's life or that she was seeing Lucy Guardino's husband, Nick Callahan, for counseling as she embarked on her new path of self-restraint and nonviolence. Well, maybe violence if circumstances called for it, but definitely nonkilling.

"You can do it." Clint's head bobbed, eyes half-closed as he imagined Morgan carrying out his orders. "Get close. Use your blade. Have fun like I taught you."

His voice turned to singsong. Good thing his hands were cuffed to the metal bar at the tabletop, otherwise they'd be down at his crotch.

"I have to go," she said, shuffling the folders and pushing the button to summon the guard.

He didn't answer, his eyes now totally closed, head weaving in time with invisible screams. Then he jerked his chin once more and opened his eyes, his stare resting on her with the pull of the sun.

No way to avoid it, no way to break free.

"Don't let me down, baby girl. You know someday I'll be out of here and we'll be together again. Together forever." The door behind him opened, and two guards entered. "You do as I say. Get the job done. Fast."

The guards unlocked his wrists from the table and pulled them behind his back, forcing him to bend forward, inches from her face. He had new wrinkles around his mouth, highlighting the pimples between the stubble of his salt-and-pepper beard. But the fiendish gleam in his eyes was enough to make her grip the edge of the table so hard her hands went numb.

Morgan held his stare without blinking or flinching. Clint was the only person on the planet who had ever inspired fear in her, and she refused to let him see it. It took all her strength to deny him that pleasure, acid filling her mouth, her throat too tight to swallow, eyes burning from not blinking.

He smiled again. Rolled his tongue across his upper teeth as if tasting an exquisite morsel.

"I'll see you soon," he promised as the guards led him away. "Real soon."

Once the door clanged shut behind him, Morgan slumped, head down onto the table, arms wrapped around her chest tight, forcing herself to stop shaking.

Should've just killed the bastard, she thought as her teeth clenched in a death grip.